THE WORLD'S WORST CHILDREN 3

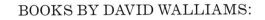

BOOKS BY DAVID WALLIAMS:

The Boy in the Dress
Mr Stink
Billionaire Boy
Gangsta Granny
Ratburger
Demon Dentist
Awful Auntie
Grandpa's Great Escape
The Midnight Gang
Bad Dad

The World's Worst Children
The World's Worst Children 2
The World's Worst Children 3

ALSO AVAILABLE IN PICTURE BOOK:

The Slightly Annoying Elephant
The First Hippo on the Moon
The Bear Who Went Boo!
The Queen's Orang-utan
There's a Snake in My School!
Boogie Bear

David Walliams

THE WORLD'S WORST CHILDREN 3

Illustrated in glorious colour by

Tony Ross

HarperCollins *Children's Books*

DAVID WALLIAMS

For
little big Albert,
with love from "Uncle" David x
D.W.

TONY ROSS

For
Wendy,
above all others
T.R.

First published in Great Britain by HarperCollins *Children's Books* in 2018
HarperCollins *Children's Books* is a division of HarperCollins*Publishers* Ltd,
HarperCollins Publishers
1 London Bridge Street
London SE1 9GF

The HarperCollins website address is
www.harpercollins.co.uk

1

ISBN 978-0-00-830460-7

THANK-YOUS

I would like to thank this collection of the world's worst grown-ups who helped me with this book.

Tony Ross, *my illustrator,* was NEVER a naughty boy. He was a wolf cub, and abided by their code. He was, however, thrown out of the scouts for curling the brim of his scout hat to make it look like John Wayne's hat.

Executive Publisher **Ann-Janine Murtagh** loved dressing up and playing with her big sister's make-up when she was little and she liked to have her cat Ossie and dog Timmy join in the fun – dressing them in ribbons and bows and putting lavish amounts of her sister's favourite lipstick on their noses!

HarperCollins CEO, **Charlie Redmayne,** once put itching powder in his sister's bed (but only after she pushed him into a clump of stinging nettles). She got a terrible rash...

My literary agent, **Paul Stevens**, once goaded his little brother into such a red-mist rage that he picked up a spoon as a weapon to attack him. Paul fled and barricaded himself into the living room for days...

My editor, **Alice Blacker,** once made a recording of scary breathing and set the recording to play in her brother's room at bedtime. She then stood by and waited for the screams of terror to come from her brother's room. And they did!

Publishing Director **Kate Burns** shared a bedroom with her sister, who had a wall full of David Cassidy posters. One day Kate decided to draw a red pen moustache on every one of the David Cassidy faces...

Publisher **Rachel Denwood** once found a hole in her parents' duvet and pulled out every single feather!

Managing Editor **Samantha Stewart** would push her vegetables through a knothole in the kitchen floor with her big toe to avoid eating her greens...

Creative Director **Val Brathwaite,** having been irritated by her little sister one too many times, decided to teach her a lesson by filling her knickers with sand...

My *PR Director*, **Geraldine Stroud,** was a champion cheater when it came to playing board games with her big brother. Her particular speciality was taking a few extra notes from the Monopoly bank when he wasn't looking!

Head of Marketing **Alex Cowan**, aged seven, persuaded his younger cousins that a glue stick was, in fact, lip gloss.

Publicist **Margot Lohan** would sneak sweets and when she got caught would scream very, very loudly until she was allowed to keep them.

My *audio editor*, **Tanya Hougham,** once painted an enormous tiger on a freshly painted wall in her parents' new house.

The world's best design team:

Sally Griffin once skipped school, only to bump straight into her headmaster – her only option was to run away from him!
Matthew Kelly decided to go fishing after school instead of doing his paper round. When discovered, he was made to deliver all the papers late at night and apologise to each person individually and with shame... **David McDougall** once spilled a can of paint on a brand-new carpet. Instead of confessing to the accident, he decided to paint over it with a different colour!

David Walliams

Hello, people of the world, and welcome to this book – in my humble view the greatest book ever written, after my own one, which was better.

It is a huge honour for me to write the introduction as my best friend in the whole world (maybe my only friend) is David **"The Dave"** Walliams. I am a big fan of all his stuff. *The World's Worst Children* is my favourite one of his books as it's mainly pictures and I only really look at the pictures.

After a long, hard day of presidential-type stuff, I often call **The Dave** for advice, and he has always had fab tips for me.

"Don't be afraid to do something different with your hair!"

"Remember, if you are the same colour as a satsuma, you are too orange!"

"Have you thought about bringing out your own presidential merchandise? The president's breakfast cereal, the president's colouring-in books, president slippers, president fidget spinners, president bubble bath, president pants? You could make a fortune!"

The Dave is big on merchandise. I always thank him for his deep spiritual wisdom.

Sometimes **The Dave** asks little old me for advice. Recently we were on holiday together in the beautiful British city of Blackpool, and we were sharing a battered sausage on the pier when **The Dave** turned to me and said, "Mr President, I am writing a sequel to *The World's Worst Children 2*, and am wracking my brain as to what I should call it. Please, please can you help?"

The pair of us sat up all night. Our heads hurt with all the thinking. We came up with title after title, but nothing seemed quite right.

- *The World's Worsterer Children*
- *The World's Worst Children 2: Part 2*
- *The World's Worst Children 2 ½*
- *The World's Worst Children Episode III: Revenge of the Sith*
- *Yet More World's Worst Children: For Goodness' Sake, When Will Walliams Give It A Rest?*
- *The World's Worst Children 4*
- *Harry Potter and the Philosopher's Stone*
- *Gangsta Granny*
- *The World's Nicest Children*
- *Monkeynuts*

Just as we were about to call it a night and admit defeat, **The Dave** came up with a genius idea.

The World's Worst Children 3!

We were both pretty sure that the number 3 followed the number 2, and it seemed like the perfect title. This just proved that **The Dave**, like me, is a genius. He then got straight on the phone to his busy ghostwriter Barbara Stoat (she even writes his shopping lists) and boom! Here it is! ***The World's Worst Children 3!***

We are still thinking about what to call the next one.

LOVE AND KISSES,
FROM THE **PRESIDENT** OF THE **UNITED STATES**
xxx

CONTENTS

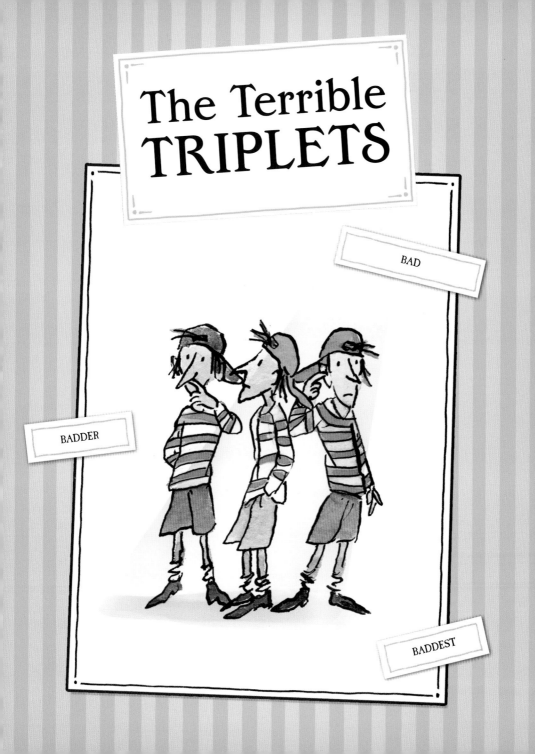

The Terrible
TRIPLETS

ONCE UPON A TIME, there was a set of terrible triplets. Their names were Tom, Dick and Harry. Sometimes when you have sets of triplets you have a mixture of nice ones and naughty ones. All three of these triplets were **naughty**.

Tom, Dick and Harry had been born just moments apart, fighting their way out of the womb, trying to elbow each other aside to see who could be first. You see, all three of them wanted to be top dog. As a result, their lives became a non-stop struggle over who was the best at something. These being three of the world's worst children, they wanted to be the best at bad things only. Very bad things.

When they were babies, Tom, Dick and Harry would battle over who could:

Bawl the loudest...

"AAAAAAAHHHHH!!!!"

Break their toys the fastest...

BASH!

Chew through the bars in their cot first...

MUNCH!

Create the most mess on the walls with their crayons...

"HA! HA!"

Soak their poor mother with the most water spat from the bath...

SPLOSH!

Flick their baby food the furthest...

SPLAT!

Wipe the most dirt from their hands on to the curtains...

W I P E !

Guzzle down the most milk...

Do the smelliest burps...

GUZZLE!

"BURP!"

PFFT!

Leave the

biggest deposit in their nappy...

When they were toddlers, the triplets

would tussle over who could:

Go **fastest** in the trolley down the supermarket aisles,

and knock over the largest number of old ladies...

WHIZZ!

Burst other children's balloons at the funfair with a drawing pin and make them cry...

POP!

Overfeed their goldfishes so they were bigger than their bowls...

"BLEURGH!"

Do the smelliest blow-offs while sitting on Father Christmas's knee...

"POOOOOOOOOOOH!"

Build the rudest snowman. This was all about where you placed the carrot...

"TEE-HEE!"

Spoil storytime by eating as many of the books as they could...

CRUNCH!

Slam the piano lid down the hardest on their nursery teacher's fingers when it was singsong time...

TWONG! "OUCH!"

Ruin another child's birthday party the **quickest**...

This might be by cheating at all the party games, opening all their presents or stuffing the **whole** birthday cake in their mouths, candles and all.

"NOOOOOOOOOOOOOOOO!"

Play the worst tricks on their father...

Tom put his father's underpants in the deep freeze so when he put them on his bottom turned blue.

"AH!"

Dick swapped his father's hair gel with **glue** so his comb became stuck to his head.

GLOOP!

Harry switched his parents' bed for a trampoline so when his father jumped on it he **bounced** right up to the ceiling and ended up clinging to the lightshade.

"HELP!"

When Tom, Dick and Harry started at school, the scraps became **fiercer** still. They would fight over who could:

SNEEZE the loudest during tests when everyone had to be silent... "AAATISSSHHOOoO!" "AATISHOO!" "AATISHHHOOo!"

Hurl **jellies** the longest distance in the school canteen...

SPLAT!

Spray their **pee** furthest from the toilet bowl – Harry managed **ten** metres...

"HOORAY!"

Boot the ball the **hardest** at the PE teacher as he refereed a football match... **"OOF!"**

Write the **crudest** thing on the school-bus window...

Get in the biggest trouble on the school trip to the local pantomime by catapulting toffees at Widow Twankey...

"OUCH!"

stinky pants
Mr plop p
Monkey breath

Ruin the Christmas carol concert
by making **monkey** noises
instead of singing...

"OoH!"

"OoH!"

"OoH!"

Cover the Art teacher in the most clay when
making a pot on the potter's wheel...

SPLAT!

Make the biggest explosion in Science class...

Tie the most children's laces together **KABOOM!**

on the start line of a running race so they **tripped** over...

"ARGH!"

Whenever this trio did something cruel to others,

they would laugh. Not a nice, happy laugh, but a mean,

mocking laugh.

"Huh! Huh! Huh!"

As you can imagine, because they were always

competing for who could be the worst of the worst,

these terrible triplets had upset absolutely everyone with whom they'd ever come in contact. And many more besides. As they grew up, Tom, Dick and Harry spent their time desperately trying to outdo each other with their *grossness*.

Tom took to eating his own **earwax**. He would spend all day and night with his little fingers in his ears, digging the smelly yellow putty out. Tom slept on the **top** bunk in the bedroom.

"SHUT UP AND LOOK AT ME!"
he would shout down.

Then to Dick and Harry's horror and delight he would eat the earwax, even though it tasted like licking a rusty climbing frame.

Dick was not to be outdone. He took to sticking his

fingers up his nose and rooting out the biggest, stickiest **bogeys** he could find stuck up there. The boy would stick the **bogeys** to each other until he had what looked like a huge green ICICLE.

Then he would shout from the **middle** bunk,

"SHUT UP AND LOOK AT ME!"

When he had his brothers' attention, he would then proceed to **suck** on the ICICLE, which tasted like a rotten cabbage lolly.

Down on the **bottom** bunk, Harry was feeling a little left out. How could he outdo the other two? Harry had a belly button that was always full of fluff. Sweaty, manky, disgusting balls of who-knew-what. As soon as he'd plucked the revolting globule out of his belly button, he shouted...

"Shut up and look at ME!"

The fluff tasted like something you might find at the bottom of a deep and dirty bog. In a word... **yucksome.**

One night, the boys' long-suffering mother stepped into their bedroom (something she tried not to do often) to read them a **nice** bedtime story.

"Hello, dear children! It's your mama!" she announced brightly. Mother was a lovely lady who smelled as **sweet** as the *delicious* cakes she baked for the local church fête. Life had delivered her a cruel blow when she gave birth to these three horrors.

The three boys all **sniggered** conspiratorially.

"Huh! Huh! Huh!"

It may come as no surprise to you that their father had long since run away from home. The poor man couldn't take the daily dose of torture any more, and had travelled as far as he possibly could, then a little bit further still. The forwarding address he left read simply:

NORTH POLE

DAD

Holding a copy of *Goldilocks and the Three Bears,*
Mother deftly **dodged** the traps the boys had laid out

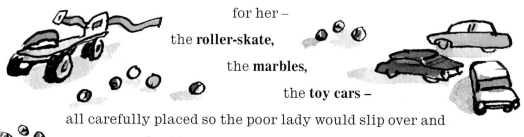

for her –

the **roller-skate,**

the **marbles,**

the **toy cars** –

all carefully placed so the poor lady would slip over and
land on her **bottom.** Mother perched tentatively on
the end of the **middle** bunk. To her **horror**, she spotted
that her middle son, Dick, was chomping on something
green and **sticky. CHOMP!**

"What on earth are you eating, dearest Richard?" she
asked.

"It's a collection of my **bogeys.** Do you want to **try?**"
The other two boys sniggered. **"Huh! Huh! Huh!"**

"No, I do not want to try!" The poor lady looked close
to tears. "For goodness' sake, why are you eating that?"

"It's one of my five a day!" he replied.

"Five a day means **fruit** or **vegetables,**
my sweetness! **Bogeys** are neither!"

"They are green, though!" said Dick.

Tom and Harry sniggered again. **"Huh! Huh! Huh!"**

"I don't care if they are green! You are not to eat your own **bogeys!"**

"How about other people's **bogeys?**" asked Dick cheekily.

"Huh! Huh! Huh!" The **top** and **bottom** bunks rocked with laughter again.

"NO!" bawled Mother. "Please! Please! Why couldn't I have had three nice boys?" she wondered aloud.

MUNCH! came a sound from the **bottom** bunk.

"Harry! What, pray tell, are you eating?"

"It's just a ball of belly-button fluff!"

"Huh! Huh! Huh!"

"Oh dear," began Mother. "Oh dear, oh dear. Oh dear, oh dear, oh dear." There weren't enough "oh dears" in the world to express how she was feeling. "And dare I ask, sweet, lovely Thomas, what you are eating?"

"Some nice fresh **earwax!**"

SLURP!

"Huh! Huh! Huh!"

Mother's nose wrinkled in **horror**. She looked close to tears. "OH! The humanity! You boys are rotters. Do you hear me? Absolute **rotters!**"

"Yeah, we **know**," replied Tom.

"Rotten rottering rottersome **rotters!**"

"I wondered why you weren't hungry at mealtimes when I serve up my *delicious* trifles – now I **know!**" began Mother. "But, boys, please mark my words." She looked at them all one by one and spoke in hushed tones. "If you eat too much of something, you will **turn into it.**"

"Yeah, right!" said Harry sarcastically.

"This is our room!" said Dick. "Get out! Boring *goody-goody* grown-ups are **not** allowed!"

"Don't you worry! I'm **going!** But, for your own good, listen to what I say," said Mother, and she spun on her heel and left. The lady hadn't allowed for the **skateboard** that had been placed right in her path. She stepped on it, and **W H I Z Z E D** across the room...

...before landing on her "**ARGH!**" *bottom* with a **THUD**.

"Goodnight, dearest Mummy!" called out the three boys in unison as the tearful lady fled out of the door.

"Huh! Huh! Huh!"

If you told Tom, Dick and Harry NOT to do something, they would do it even more. Their whole lives were a **competition** to see who could be the worst of the worst. The worstest.

The worsterest.

The worsterestestest.

This was the triplets' chance to find out once and for all who was the grossest of the three. So they began storing their chosen **"foods"** in larger and larger quantities.

Tom began to stockpile his **earwax**, keeping it in an empty jigsaw box at the end of his bed.

Dick picked and picked and picked his nose, and stuck all his **bogeys** to each other. Soon he had a **bogey** stalactite as tall as he was.

Harry collected his balls of belly-button **fluff**, and placed them in a **chocolate box.** This plan went awry when their elderly grandmother visited and assumed they were indeed chocolates, and scoffed the lot.

"These chocolates taste **hairy**," she muttered as she plopped another in her mouth.

"Huh! Huh! Huh!" the three laughed.

With all his own balls of belly-button **fluff** gone, Harry went to all the **grubbiest** boys in his school and plucked out theirs.

"GIMME THAT!"

"GET **OFF!**"

"I WANT YOUR **FLUFF!**"

"OUCH!"

"JUST HOLD STILL!"

"LEAVE MY **BELLY BUTTON** ALONE, YOU BRUTE!"

So, with these added "donations", Harry soon had a full box of **stomach-churning** delights.

Finally, the three boys were ready to begin their **scoffing** competition. The feast was to be at midnight. They slid out of their bunk beds, and tiptoed down the stairs. They took their places round the kitchen table, three big plates of their repulsive foods in front of them.

As the clock in the hallway chimed midnight, the race began.

Tom **munched** his way through the mountain of **earwax**.

"LOOK AT **ME!**" he declared.

"I AM THE GROSSEST OF US **ALL!**"

Dick devoured a **bogey** that was nearly as **big** as he was.
"NO, NO, NO!" said Dick.

"LOOK AT **ME**! I AM SO GROSS I MAKE YOU
LOOK LIKE *Goldilocks!*"

Meanwhile Harry scoffed a whole box of fluff balls.

"THE TWO OF YOU ARE NOTHING BUT A PAIR OF
goody gumdrops! BOW DOWN BEFORE **ME**,
THE GROSSEST BOY WHO EVER
WALKED THE **EARTH**!"

This was the most repulsive midnight feast **ever** and, despite all their bravado, the three boys began to feel quite *ill*.

As the boys ate and ate and ate, the **strangest** thing happened.

Slowly Tom's **skin** began turning yellow. Soon he was not just yellow, but also shiny, just like the **earwax** he was devouring.

1.   2.   3.

Meanwhile Dick was turning as green as the **INCREDIBLE HULK**. However, unlike the **INCREDIBLE HULK**, Dick was becoming

1.   2.   3.

disgustingly **sticky.**

As for Harry, he was slowly turning into a giant ball of fluff. HAIR was sprouting everywhere. He even had hair growing out of his hair.

1.   2.   3.

The terrible triplets were so intent on munching as much as they could, as fast as they could, that they **didn't** notice what was happening to them.

MUNCH! GULP!

SLURP!

"I CAN EAT THE **FASTEST!**" bragged Tom.

"I CAN EAT THE **MOST!**" bragged Dick.

"I CAN EAT THE **MOST** THE **FASTEST!**" bragged Harry.

MUNCH!

GULP! SLURP!

They raced and **raced** through their snacks of **DOOM.**

"FINISHED!" shouted the three boys in unison.

"IT'S A DEAD **HEAT!**" yelled Tom.

"WE ARE AS GROSS AS EACH OTHER!" added Dick.

"BUT WE **HAVE** TO BE THE GROSSEST

CHILDREN IN THE WORLD!" concluded Harry.

"Huh! **Huh! Huh!**" they all sniggered together. After all that scoffing, the three felt more than a little **unwell,** though nobody wanted to admit it. They went back to their bunk beds **farting** and **burping**...

...hoping the **awful** feeling coming from their tummies would have worn off by the morning.

How **wrong** they were.

At seven o'clock their mother knocked on their bedroom door.

"Wakey-wakey! *Rise and shine!* Time to get **up,** my angels!" she called out brightly.

One by one, the three boys began to stir.

From the **top** bunk, Tom peered down to Dick. He couldn't believe his eyes. Pointing at his brother, he burst out laughing.

"Huh! Huh! Huh!"

"WOT?" demanded Dick.

"You look like a humongous bogey!" replied Tom.

"Do I?" said Dick. "Well, you look like a great big globule of earwax!"

"Do I?"

"Yes, you do!" chimed in Harry. "You both look like something from a *HORROR* movie! Huh! Huh! Huh!" A smug expression fixed on his face.

"I would wipe that smile **off** your face if I were you!" said Tom.

"Why?" asked Harry.

"Because you have turned into a giant ball of belly-button fluff! Huh! Huh! Huh!" replied Dick.

The three boys **darted** out of their bedroom to the bathroom.

They all wrestled for a look at themselves in the mirror.

"**ARGH!**" they screamed in unison.

In no time, their mother rushed into the bathroom.

"Oh dear! Oh dear, oh dear! What are you yelling about now?" she demanded. As soon as she caught a glimpse of her sons, she screamed too.

"**ARGH!**"

The three boys felt very sorry for themselves and, in unison, burst into **tears**.

"WHA-HAA!"

"Mummy!" began Tom. "Help me! I am a giant piece of **earwax!**"

"Help me, Mummy! I am a great big **bogey!**" confessed Dick.

"Mummy, Mummy, please, please help **me!** I am **half** boy, **half** belly-button fluff," blubbed Harry.

Mother studied her youngest son for a moment.

"I would say you were a **quarter** boy, three-quarters belly-button fluff!"

Harry's bottom lip quivered, and tears **streamed** down his furry face. "Now I am not just hairy. I am wet and hairy! **WHAA!**"

Mother shook her head and sighed. "You didn't listen, did you? Now, **what** did I tell you?"

The triplets thought for a moment.

"Don't tie next-door's cat's tail to the newspaper boy's bicycle?" guessed Tom.

"No," replied Mother.

"Don't burn all your dresses in a bonfire as a joke?" guessed Dick.

"No," said Mother. "Not specifically that, but obviously please, please, please **don't** do that again."

"I've got it!" announced Harry. **"Don't** swap the Rice Krispies with gravel!"

"NO!" snapped Mother loudly. It was **so** loud she **SHOCKED** herself. "Oh dear. Now, where was I? Yes, I said, 'If you eat too much of something, you will turn into it.' "

"Oh yeah," they replied in unison. They weren't the smartest of children.

"Now, come on, boys! It's time to get ready for school."

"We **can't** go to school like this!" protested Tom.

"We look rɪdɪcuɪous!" added Dick.

"We will be a **laughing stock!**" begged Harry.

"That is what I am hoping!" said Mother with a wicked glint in her eye. "Come along! Chop-chop!"

As the lady led her terrible triplets into the playground that morning, the entire school turned round. They couldn't believe their **eyes.**

"Look! A giant **bogey boy!**"

shouted one child on seeing Dick.

"And a great big shaft of **earwax!**"

hollered another, pointing at Tom.

"NO! NO! **LOOK!**

A huge hairy ball of

belly-button fluff!"

bellowed a third, indicating Harry.

The terrible triplets were now as revolting as each other. Needless to say, all the children in the playground, who had all been **TERRORISED** by the three boys over the years, burst out laughing. They laughed. And laughed. And laughed.

"Huh! Huh! Huh!" laughed the children.

Tom, Dick and Harry had to stand there and take it. At last they'd had a taste of their own medicine.

TANDY'S
Tantrums

Tantrums ARE SOMETHING toddlers have. When they don't get their own way, they scream and cry. It is a stage children grow out of.

Not Tandy.

The little girl had tantrums all day, **every** day.

It had been like that ever since she was a baby. Back then, **anything** could set a **tantrum** off – having her **dummy** taken away, going over a **bump** in her pram, not having enough **milk** to guzzle. Sometimes, baby Tandy would have a **tantrum** just because it had been a while since she'd had a **tantrum**. As a toddler, Tandy could **scream** and **cry** louder than an entire stadium full of children.

It was so loud, in fact, that when she screamed and cried grown-ups **always** gave in to her. And every time a grown-up gave in to her Tandy realised that her **tantrums** worked.

At the time our story begins, Tandy was eleven years old and having hundreds of tantrums every day. They were so unbearable that whatever Tandy wanted Tandy got.

"What's for pudding?" the girl would demand every night after dinner.

Mother and Father would look at each other, concerned. They knew what was coming.

"Well, my angel sent from heaven, I thought as you had ice cream last night," began Mother, "and the night before that, and the night before that, and the night before that—"

"In fact, every night in living memory, O beauteous daughter of mine," interrupted Father.

"That tonight it might be a good idea to have some –"

Mother winced as she said it –

"fruit."

The little girl stared at them.

"**FRUIT?**"

Her eyes flickered with **fury.**

"**FRUIT?!**"

First, her bottom lip began to **quiver,** then her top.

"**FRUIT?!!**"

Then her face began to turn the colour of an **angry beetroot.**

"**FRUIT?!!!**"

Next, her hair began to stand **ON END.**

"**FRUIT?!!!!**"

Then she took a deep breath and let out a scream...

"WHHHAAA!"

... so terrible that:

People's spectacles cracked...

CRACK! CRUNCH!

Melons exploded...

KABooM!

Birds fell out of the trees, stone dead...

DOOF!

Plates flew off shelves and smashed on the ground...

Buses skidded off the road...

SCREECH!

CRASH!

Garden sheds collapsed...

THUD!

Earwax melted and splurged out of people's ears...

SPLURT!

Cats' fur fell out...

"MIAOW!"

Books caught fire... **WOOF!**

Cathedrals crumbled...

CRUNCH!

CRACK!

"NOOO!" her parents screamed as they plugged their ears with their fingers in a desperate attempt to block out the noise.

"**WHAAAAAAA!** I HATE **FRUIT!**" Tandy wailed.

"PLEASE, DARLING DAUGHTER!" pleaded Mother, shouting over the **din.**

But there was no stopping the girl.

"**WHAAAAAAAAAAA!**"

"Just one little piece of fruit, my speck of stardust! Please try it! You might like it!" implored Father. He handed her a grape from the bowl.

There was calm for a moment as Tandy's **tantrum** stopped, and she placed the grape in her mouth. Mother and Father shared a tentative smile. It was to be in vain. The girl spat the grape back at her father.

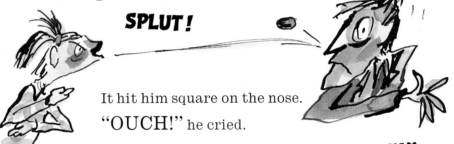

SPLUT!

It hit him square on the nose.
"OUCH!" he cried.

"WHHHHAAAAAAA! I HATE GRAPES!"

"Well, if you don't like grapes, how about a banana, my ray of sunshine?" said Mother, hastily peeling one. She handed the fruit to her daughter. Once again, she put it in her mouth before firing it straight back at her mother. It hit her bang in the eye.

BOOF!

"OW!" shrieked Mother.

Tandy was quite the spitter. This week alone she'd spat back a pear, some pineapple chunks, a strawberry and a kumquat. Father hated the waste, so put it all in the compost heap at the end of the garden.

"WHHHHHHAAAAAA! I HATE BANANAS!"

The house began shaking at the noise of Tandy's tantrum. It was as if there were an **earthquake** hitting. The cutlery on the table started rattling.

CLANK!

CLUNK!

The lemonade in the glasses began bubbling and frothing.

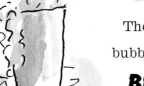

BLURB!

SPLURGE!

Ketchup spurted out of the bottle, repainting the ceiling red.

KETCHUP

Pictures fell off the walls and **smashed** on

the floor.

SHATTER!

The goldfish leaped out of its

bowl, and landed on the carpet.

SPLUT!

It flapped around there for

a few moments before Father placed it back in its bowl,

where it buried itself under some gravel. **DIG!**

Soon snot was flying out of the girl's nose like water

from a hose. **WHOOSH!**

Mother and Father were soaked.

"PLEASE! USE A TISSUE!" begged Mother.

"WHHHHHHAAAAAAA!

I HATE **TISSUES!**"

"WELL, THEN USE YOUR NAPKIN,

MY GOLDEN GIRL SENT FROM ABOVE!"

implored Father.

"WHHHHHHHHAAAAAAA! I HATE **NAPKINS**.

I WOULD MUCH RATHER DRENCH YOU

BOTH IN **SNOT!** NOW GIVE ME MY ICE CREAM! NOW!"

Reluctantly, Mother and Father scurried off to the

kitchen to do the little girl's

bidding. Not taking any

chances, the pair of them returned as fast as they could with a huge bowl of **ice cream**.

"Forgive us for the delay, O rainbow child," said Mother. Concerned about what flavour their **darling** daughter might want, they gave her a dollop of every one they had: **vanilla, chocolate, mint choc-chip, caramel, fudge, double fudge** and cookie-dough surprise.

"Here you go, gorgeous!" announced Mother. "Your ice cream!"

"WHHHHHHHHHHAAAAAAAAAAAA!"

"WHAT NOW, MY FURRY KITTEN?" demanded Father.

"I WANT A **FLAKE!** AND **CHOCOLATE SAUCE!** AND ANOTHER **FLAKE!**"

Father scurried back into the kitchen as Mother placed the ice cream down in front of her daughter.

"There you go, O cherub of the skies. The flakes and chocolate sauce won't be a mo!"

The woman spoon-fed her daughter a huge mouthful. "That might shut you up for a while," said Mother, forgetting herself for a moment. "O songbird of love."

"wHHHHHHHAAAAAAAA!" the girl wailed as she **spat** the ice cream across the table, covering her mother's face with it.

"Oh, what is wrong, my angel delight?"

"I HATE ICE CREAM WITHOUT FLAKES OR CHOCOLATE SAUCE! WHHHHHHAAAAAAAAA!"

"Here it comes, my sweet nectar!" called out Father as he rushed back into the room.

The man stuck the flakes into his daughter's ice cream, and then *squirted* chocolate sauce over it.

"Say when, honey blossom..." he prompted.

The entire bottle of chocolate sauce was emptied over the ice cream until there was only chocolatey air coming out.

"When," said Tandy.

"Super-duper, my floppy-eared bunny!" said Father.

Tandy shovelled some ice cream into her mouth.

"We got there!" she mumbled.

Mother and Father shared a **sigh** of relief.

The next morning on his way to work, Father passed some men digging a hole in the road. They were using a huge mechanical drill, which made an **awful** racket, though not as awful as his daughter's tantrums.

DDDDDRRRRRR!

He noticed that the road-workers were using noise-cancelling headphones, and had a **bright idea! DING!**

That afternoon, he returned from his day at the office with a present for his wife. "There you are, my darling wife!"

"What's this, husband?" she asked excitedly. The lady unwrapped the package to find two pairs of headphones.

"His and hers!" said Father.

"What a **splendiferous** idea!" said Mother.

"Where is our dearest darling daughter?"

"She is upstairs in her bedroom watching **cartoons.** She has lots of homework to do, but..."

"She threw one of her little **tantrumettes?**" he asked with a wry smile.

"How did you guess, my perfect husband?"

"Well, let's see how we get on with these tonight," said Father, putting on his **headphones.**

"Yes, let's!" replied Mother.

"What did you say?" asked Father.

"Sorry, I can't hear a word," replied Mother.

The pair sat down in the living room and read, delighted to be enjoying some peace and quiet for once. Father read some poetry, while Mother read a travel book. Her *dream* was to travel **far** away, somewhere where she couldn't hear her daughter **SCREAM.**

What they didn't hear with their **headphones** on was their daughter bawling for her dinner from upstairs.

"WHHHHHAAAAAA! FOOOOD!"

Eventually Tandy had no choice but to **stomp** all the way downstairs and confront them.

"WHHHAAAAAAAA! I **WANT** MY DINNER! NOOOOW!"

The two grown-ups held their nerve, and carried on reading.

"WHHHAAAAAAAAAAA! I **HATE** YOU SO MUCH!"

"If you ask nicely, my roll of **extra-soft** toilet tissue, then we will take these off," said Father, indicating his headphones.

"WHHHAAAAAAAAAAAA! I HATE ASKING NICELY!"

"I am sorry, my cream-cake princess," began Mother. "We can't hear you."

"WHHHAAAAAAAAAAAAAA! I AM STARVING!"

With that, Tandy plucked the **goldfish** out of its bowl by its tail, and dropped it in her mouth.

"NOOO!" yelled Father.

"Spit it out, my sparkling diamond!" shouted Mother.

With a grin, the girl spat the goldfish back into its bowl.

"WHHHAAAAAA! I WANT MY DINNER!"

"Quieter, please, my dollop of blancmange!" prompted Father, lifting up one headphone to hear.

"WHHAAAA! I want my dinner!"

"Now try it without the WHAAA."

"I want my dinner!"

"What's the *magic* word, sweetest pea?" asked Mother.

"Abracadabra?" replied Tandy.

"No. As you and I well know, it is 'please'."

"Please," mumbled the girl.

"Now pop that word into a sentence, Miss Candyfloss!"

"I **want** my dinner..." Tandy hesitated. This was hard. "...please."

"See! We got there in the end!" said Father.

"Harrumph!" harrumphed Tandy.

However, little did the grown-ups know that their daughter was hatching a *devilish* plan. If Mother and Father were going to continue wearing headphones, and by the **smug** looks on their faces it was clear they were **not** going to give them up any time soon, Tandy's tantrums just had to become **LOUDER.** MUCH **LOUDER.**

The girl lived not far from a **huge** stadium that was home to football matches and rock concerts. One Saturday afternoon, she crept out of the house and cycled there. A **huge** poster outside the stadium advertised that night's entertainment. It was a rock band from the 1960s called the **Rollicking Fossils**, and they were playing their "15th & Final Farewell Tour".

Parked outside the stadium was a fleet of **huge**
lorries. Tandy ducked and dived around them and
saw that one contained a **huge** speaker the size of
a small bungalow. This was designed to deliver a
DEAFENING noise to 150,000 people, and
was sure to do the trick.

There was **no** way those noise-cancelling
headphones could cancel out
this beast.

So, while no one was looking, she loaded her bike into the back of the **lorry** and climbed up into the cab. Next, despite having **never** had a driving lesson, she **drove** the lorry all the way back to her house, **DEMOLISHING** hundreds of vehicles as she swerved around the road.

BANG!

CRASH!

ROLLICKING FOSSILS

WALLOP!

Eventually she **smashed** the lorry into her next-door neighbour's house...

BASH!

...and pushed the speaker down the ramps and into her front garden.

TRUNDLE!

Then she connected a **microphone** up to the speaker, and stood in front of it. With the **microphone** in hand, she launched into a **tantrum** the likes of which had never been heard before.

"WHHHHHHAAA!"

The speaker was meant to amplify the sound of an electric guitar. An electric guitar was much quieter than one of Tandy's **tantrums.**

QUIET

| FLEA'S FART | LEAF BLOWING IN THE BREEZE | ELEPHANT'S TRUNK TRUMPETING | ELECTRIC GUITAR | SEAL BARKING | PRIME MINISTER'S QUESTIONS AT THE HOUSE OF COMMONS | THUNDER |

The noise from the speaker made Tandy's tantrum SO UNBELIEVABLY **LOUD** that it created a gigantic **SOUND WAVE** that propelled Tandy forward at **speed.**

LOUD

OLD LADY AT THE BINGO
HALL SHOUTING, "BINGO!" HIPPOPOTAMUS BLOWING OFF VOLCANO EXPLODING ONE OF TANDY'S TANTRUMS

The girl **smashed** through the living-room window...

...and **flew** past her parents, who were **quietly**
reading.

"ARGH!" Tandy **SCREAMED,** but they didn't hear
her. They didn't hear her **smash** through the **window** at
the back of the house either.

However, Mother did notice the **sudden** draught, and looked up from her book. The lady was horrified to see her daughter's legs sticking out of the compost heap at the back of the garden. She yanked off her headphones, and **grabbed** her husband.

"Look, love of my life!"

The pair dashed outside, and pulled their daughter out of the compost. She had bits of **WASTE** all over her face. The banana she'd **SPAT** back at her mother was now tangled in her hair.

"WHAA!" she cried for a moment before stopping herself.

"What on earth happened, pony princess?" asked Father.

"I had a **tantrum** that went badly **wrong**, so I am having a **tantrum** about that. **WHHAA!**"

"You are having a **tantrum** about a **tantrum**, honey monster?" said Mother.

"Yes. **WHHHAAA!**"

Mother and Father looked at each and **sighed**. "Shall we move to Australia?" he asked.

"We've always talked about it, O husband of joy."

"**Right now**, wife of my heart?"

"No time like the **present**, raindrop of love."

Father took Mother's hand and they walked back through the house.

"Goodbye, sweet angel sent from above to ruin our lives!" they called out to their daughter.

"**WHHHHHAAAAA!**"

cried Tandy.

They **never** saw their daughter again. Though sometimes, while lying in bed at night in Australia, they swore they could hear Tandy on the other side of the world having one of her titanic **tantrums.**

But unfortunately for Tandy there was **no one** there to run to her.

Boastful
BARNABUS

BIG HEAD THAT CAN
ONLY GET BIGGER

POSHEST SCHOOL
UNIFORM ON EARTH

TOO MANY CUPS,
MEDALS AND PRIZES

Boastful
BARNABUS

BARNABUS WAS A BOY who loved to boast. In his own way, he was one of the world's very worst children.

The tall, lolloping boy came from an extremely **posh** family, and he wanted you to know it. Barnabus was a pupil at  a five-hundred-year-old school set in a thousand acres of English countryside.

The fees were **£100,000** a year, all the boys had to wear bow ties and top hats, and there was only one old boy who hadn't gone on to become a prime minister or **king**. The most he'd managed was to become the foreign secretary. As he'd brought great shame on the school, his name was removed from the long list of ex-pupils whose names were painted in **gold leaf** on the huge wooden boards that hung in the cavernous entrance hall.

Whilst speed walking from one dusty old classroom to another, carrying his monogrammed leather briefcase, Barnabus would pull boys aside in the corridor to boast about his latest achievement.

"Tarquin!" he called after a boy one frosty morning.

"Oh yes, Barnabus?" replied Tarquin eagerly, his little round spectacles steaming up at being in the presence of the golden boy of the entire school.

"The Mathematics test results have just been put up on the board. There is **good** news and **bad** news."

"Do tell!"

Barnabus pursed his lips. "The **bad news** is I only received **ninety-nine per cent**. I will have to have words with the Mathematics master, Mr Troughton, as to why I was marked down a whole **one** per cent."

"Congratulations, Barnabus! Pray tell, what is the **good news?**"

Barnabus smirked. He was going to enjoy this. "The good news, Tarquin, is that you failed, with a measly **forty-nine per cent!**"

"Oh dear!" Poor Tarquin's face clouded with worry.

"So every cloud has a silver lining! Good day!" said Barnabus, and he swept his scarf round his neck theatrically, slapping poor Tarquin on the nose.

"OOF!"

The strangest thing was that every time Barnabus boasted about something his head became a tiny bit **bigger.** Barnabus was oblivious to this, and would complain again and again to his housemaster in his office. Mr Hartnell was as antique as his furniture. Both dated back to Victorian times.

"Mr Hartnell! Someone has shrunk my top hat!"

The teacher examined the silk topper in detail, and placed it on his own head for reference.

"Don't do that!" chided Barnabus. "You might have **nits**."

"Apologies, Barnabus. Have you considered that your head might be becoming **bigger?**"

"NONSENSE!"

thundered Barnabus. "Now you may go!"

"But it's **my** office!" protested the teacher.

"Well, I want **you** to go anyway."

Poor old Mr Hartnell shrugged, and shuffled out of the room.

"As quick as you can, please!"

snapped Barnabus, and his teacher trundled off as fast as his little old legs could carry him.

The big-headed boy didn't just excel in his lessons – he was a fine sportsman too.

One morning, the Games master, Mr Pertwee, announced the name of the new school cricket captain.

"After lengthy trials, and much careful consideration—" began Pertwee.

"Don't go on and on, sir. I think we all know it's me!" shouted out Barnabus.

"– our new cricket captain is Barnabus!"

In that moment, the big-headed boy's head **expanded** just a little, and his top hat was squeezed off his head.

It shot up and hit the ceiling.

PING!

THWAT!

"Stupid small hat," muttered Barnabus. "Now, three cheers for me! Hip hip!"

"Hooray!" said the rest of the school wearily.

"Louder, please. Hip hip!"

"Hooray!"

"Louder still. Hip hip!"

"HOORAY!"

"That sounded sarcastic. One more for luck. Hip hip!"

"HOORAY!"

"Oh, and by the way, as captain of the cricket team, I am dismissing all the other players. I will play all positions myself.

Thank you so much!"

It was the same story with the school play. It wasn't enough for Barnabus to be awarded the title role in Shakespeare's *Hamlet* – he wanted to play all the parts himself.

At the very first rehearsal, he announced, "All the other actors may go. I am such a magnificent actor that I will play every role. This is to be the first ever ONE-MAN *Hamlet!*"

"But, Barnabus!" spluttered Mr Tennant, the Drama teacher.

"No buts, sir. You are relieved too. I will direct myself!"

In the end, Barnabus even wrote his own review in the school magazine, THE CUTHBERTIAN.

It read:

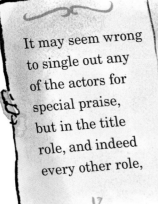

It may seem wrong to single out any of the actors for special praise, but in the title role, and indeed every other role, Barnabus was outstanding. Without doubt, the end-of-year school acting prize should go to me, I mean him.

17

Prize-giving Day was always Barnabus's favourite day of the year. This particular year, the boy was determined that he should win all the prizes. Every. Single. One.

The headmaster, Mr Baker, stood on the stage in front of the entire school. Behind him was an array of **silver cups**, all waiting to be awarded to those who'd been the **best** at something.

The first prize of the afternoon was for attendance. This is one that you win if you never miss a day of school. Barnabus was so determined to win this that, even though he had contracted tonsillitis and had to have his tonsils removed, he'd made the surgeon do it in the middle of a History lesson so he would **not** miss a moment of school.

Kings who
went to
this school:
Richard III
Henry VIII
George III

"The attendance prize goes to… Barnabus!" announced Mr Baker.

The boy's head **expanded** noticeably as he waltzed up on to the stage to collect it.

"The Mathematics prize goes to…

Barnabus!"

The boy's buttocks had barely brushed his seat before he was up again to collect the second award. Once again, his head **expanded**. All the boys began muttering and pointing as Barnabus waltzed back on to the stage.

As the sound of Mr Hartnell snoring at the back echoed around the hall –

"ZZZZ! ZZZZ! ZZZZ! ZZZZ!"

– more and more awards were announced.

By the **twentieth** award, the Drama prize (which Barnabus won by default as he was the only boy who'd stepped on the school stage that year), the boy's head was beginning to look utterly **bizarre**.

It was now the size of a **beach ball**, so big that his glasses pinged off, and his head **wobbled** on his neck.

Yet again he breezed back up on to the stage. His strange appearance provoked titters from the boys in the audience.

"Ha ha!"

The headmaster wore very thick glasses. His eyesight was so poor he didn't notice. As for Barnabus, he was so hungry to collect every single prize that he hadn't noticed either. The Drama prize was a silver figure of a Shakespearean character wielding a sharp sword.

As more and more prizes were announced, Barnabus began dropping trophies as he made his way back to the stage.

CLUNK!

CLANG!

THUD!

It was impossible to keep hold of all of them, and each time his head would get that bit **bigger**, as if someone were blowing air into a balloon. Now it was the size of an igloo.

Oblivious, Mr Baker carried on with the awards. He announced the last but one prize of the afternoon.

"The chess prize goes to...

Tarquin!"

A **huge** cheer went up around the school as at least one prize wasn't going to Barnabus.

When a delighted Tarquin rose from his seat, Barnabus bellowed,

"WHAT IS THE MEANING OF THIS?"

"What do you mean, what is the meaning of this?" asked the headmaster.

"Why haven't I won the chess prize, you **buffoon?**"

Tarquin popped his hand up. "If I might interject here, sir? I think, Barnabus, it's for the simple reason that you never came to Chess Club. It clashes with Drama Society. So, I am sorry to say, you couldn't do both."

Barnabus's **giant** head turned a violent shade of **red.**

"But if I'd come to Chess Club then without doubt I would have been the **bestest** at it."

"Can you play chess, Barnabus?" asked Tarquin.

"I never have, but I am sure if I did I would **win.** So the chess prize should go to ME!"

"Please, please, Barnabus, don't make a scene!" begged the headmaster. "There is still one more prize to go, remember. Now, Tarquin, please come up to the stage to collect your prize."

Little Tarquin beamed with pride as the entire school gave him a **standing ovation.**

"Well done, boy!" muttered the headmaster as he handed over the **smallest** silver cup.

"Thank you, sir!"

"CHEAT!" shouted Barnabus.

Undeterred, Tarquin approached Barnabus on the way back to his seat. "I apologise, Barnabus. Maybe next year this will be yours."

Barnabus went to snatch the cup. "I'll take it **now!**"

Tarquin whisked it out of the way just in time. "And, Barnabus?"

"What is it, you cheat?"

"I am worried about your head."

"What about my head?"

"It's become really **big**. Maybe you need to go and see Matron and have a lie-down in the sick bay!"

"And **miss** the final prize?" thundered Barnabus. **"NEVER!** Now come on, Headmaster, you great Heffalump. Get a move on!"

"So it's time to find out which St Cuthbert's boy has won the most coveted prize of all. That of being made head boy of the **entire school!**"

A murmur of excitement echoed around the school hall.

"OOOOOOOOH!"

Mr Baker cleared his throat. "Ha-hum. The new head boy of St Cuthbert's is—"

"GET ON WITH IT, YOU **CHUMP!**"

bellowed Barnabus.

"Barnabus!"

Barnabus's head

expanded

to the size of a

hot-air

balloon.

Clinging to his numerous cups and trophies, he tripped on his way up to the stage to collect his final prize. He dropped his haul, including the Drama prize.

CLANK!

BING!

CLATTER!

"HA! HA!" laughed the whole school.

Barnabus fell forward, and the tiny sword the figure was holding became embedded in the boy's **swollen** forehead.

SPLUT!

"HELP!" screamed Barnabus. He hated pain unless he was inflicting it on others.

Of course, the headmaster didn't see the boy. He tripped over him and fell off the stage, much to the mirth of all the schoolboys. **"HA! HA!"**

Being the nice one, Tarquin leaped up to help. First, he aided the elderly headmaster to his feet.

"Thank you, **madam**," muttered Mr Baker.

"Don't worry about that old wombat! What about ME?" demanded Barnabus.

"Yes, of course, of course!" said Tarquin, and he rushed up on to the stage to help his tormentor.

"Pull the blasted thing out!" demanded Barnabus.

"Are you sure?"

"Of course I am sure!"

"I'm just worried that something might go horribly wrong."

"What are you talking about, you imbecilic imbecile?

PULL IT OUT!

NOW!"

Tarquin did what he was told, and pulled the little
sword out of the boy's **humongous** head.
It was exactly like popping a balloon.

BOOM!

There was this **huge** sound, like a giant's fart, as
hot air rushed out of Barnabus's bonce. *PFFT!*

The balloon boy **shot** across the school hall, and bounced off the ceiling and walls before **ZOOMING** out of an open window.

The whole school pressed their faces up to the glass to watch as Barnabus flew UP into the air and **exploded** over the cricket field.

BANG!

It was SO loud it even woke up the boy's housemaster, Mr Hartnell.

"Did I miss anything?" asked the teacher, waking up with a start.

"Nothing of note," remarked Mr Pertwee, who was sitting next to him. "Except that the new head boy became so **big-headed** he actually exploded."

"Jolly good!" muttered Hartnell before he went back to sleep.

"ZZZZ, ZZZZ!"

"ZZZZZ, ZZZZZ!"

FANNY'S
Funny Faces

Fanny was a girl who delighted in **pulling faces.**
She had a huge number in her collection:

The simple **"gurn"**...

The **"Bus driver, will you please open the doors?"**...

The *"hog"*...

The **"fish-face"**...

The "flappy"...

The **"postbox"**...

The *"walnut"*...

The **"I have swallowed my pencil!"**...

The *"balloon"*...

The **"Do I need braces?"**...

The *"troll"*...

It was as if her face were made of rubber and she could **contort** it in **every** way imaginable. Of course, there is nothing wrong with pulling **funny faces** in the privacy of your own home. To lock yourself in the bathroom, stand in front of the mirror and contort your face into something **MONSTROUS** is a wonderful way to spend an evening.

However, Fanny took these **funny faces** outside to unleash them on the world.

You see, Fanny **loved** to **shock.**

She **loved** to **APPAL.**

Most of all, she **loved** to **HORRIFY.**

One time, Fanny hid behind a hedge near the local church. There she held her breath until her face went bright red like a **devil,** before **leaping** out to shock the local vicar.

"HELP!"
he cried.

The man was

SO frightened

he scrambled

up the drainpipe on the side

of his church and ended

up clinging to the spire.

He **actually** stayed there for

THREE MONTHS.

Another time, Fanny climbed a tree in the local park. There she waited until an old lady passed underneath, walking her little dog on a lead. Fanny swung upside down with her arms folded, baring her fangs in her best "vampire" face. The poor old dear shrieked in terror.

"ARGH!"

Her little dog was so scared that it scuttled off, dragging its owner at speed across the grass.

"HHHEEEEELLLP!"

"WOOF! WOOF!"

That little old lady was eventually found in a field **200 miles away.**

However, Fanny's finest funny face was when she fooled her **whole** school into thinking she had a contagious disease. She jutted out her chin, narrowed her eyes and took a swig of **bubble bath** so she started foaming at the mouth.

Then she ran round in circles in the playground

HOWLING,

"WOO! HOO! HOO!"

The teachers shoved the pupils out of the way as they
desperately tried to flee. The headmistress was the worst –

she picked up the smaller children

and **HURLED** them at the
RABID BEAST,

hoping it would bite them and **not** her.

The school was shut down for months while an army of people in airtight outfits sprayed everything in sight with **disinfectant.**

This included the caretaker, who, in fairness, had always needed **disinfecting.**

"Thank you. I won't need a bath now for another couple of years," he was heard to mutter.

It is needless to say that Fanny's father was furious when he found out about the **mayhem** his little girl had been causing.

"No more funny faces, Fanny!" he **THUNDERED.**
The man was **so** angry that his face went purple and his eyes crossed.

Fanny just mimicked him. She **slapped** her cheeks and crossed her eyes.

"*No more funny faces, Fanny!*" she shouted.

"Don't just **repeat** everything I say!" bawled Fanny's father.
"*Don't just repeat everything I say!*" **repeated** Fanny.

"And stop pulling that funny face!"

"*And stop pulling that* funny face!"

Fanny's father was **so** furious that he **glowed** even more purple, and his eyes went even **more** crossed.

"Mark my words, young lady!" he began. "One day the wind will change and you will get **STUCK** like that!"
One day it did.

Our story begins on an **ordinary** morning. Fanny was in the bathroom, where she'd been putting the finishing touches to some new **funny faces**:

The "**tongue stuck up nose**"…

The "**Who blew off?**"…

The "**I've sat on a scorpion**"…

The "**toothless**"…

The "**Bleurgh!**"…

The "**looking at yourself in a spoon**"…

The "**monocle**"…

The "**cauliflowers for ears**"…

The "**hundred chins**"…

Finally Fanny settled on one she liked: the "bottom-faced girl". She achieved this by pursing her lips and blowing out her cheeks at the same time. This gave the appearance that she'd undergone a bottom/face transplant, and that during some BIZARRE operation her face had been swapped with her bottom.*

* Other transplants that come highly unrecommended include: hand to foot, neck to leg, belly button to mouth, nose to chin, ear to elbow, head to knee, back to front.

Fanny studied herself in the mirror. Her eyes lit up with glee. This was her **MASTERPIECE!** It would place her in the history books as the **GREATEST FACE-PULLER OF ALL TIME**. There was quite some competition. The top face-pullers in the world were:

A hairy rock guitarist from Los Angeles called **Zonk** who was famed for **contorting** his face and beard into a "monkey's **armpit**"...

A boy from Germany named **Heinz Heinz** who did an internationally acclaimed "kitten in a **washing machine**"...

A hundred-year-old lady from China, Ming Mang Mung, whose speciality was "the dried **prune**"...

A round-faced Indian man named Harish Patel who did a mighty **"Frisbee"**...

A Japanese sumo wrestler named Miko the Mountain who did a surprisingly moving "hippopotamus sitting on the toilet"...

Monsieur Franglais from France who won gold in the French **Face-pulling** Championships for his face like a "bag of spanners"... (It turned out he **wasn't** pulling a face, after all, but actually looked like that.)

Concetta Castonetta, a girl from **Mexico** who, with the help of some green paint, cocktail sticks and glue, did a "cactus" so well that a dog did a pee up against her...

Baba, an unusually large baby from Vladivostok, who won a number of **face-pulling** trophies for his disturbing "boy trapped under the ice"...

Sheik Itallabout from Saudi Arabia who did a world-class "disgruntled camel"...

Khalid, a disgruntled camel from Saudi Arabia, who did a world-class "Sheik Itallabout"...

This particular "bottom-faced girl" expression of Fanny's was **special**. It deserved to be seen by as many people as possible. The girl decided to take herself and her face all the way to London. In the city, there were **hundreds**, **thousands**, even **millions** of people to shock, appal and horrify.

As soon as she stepped on to the train that morning, folk fled in **FEAR.**

"AAH !"

"NOOO!"

"SHE HAS A BOTTOM FOR A FACE!"

"WHAT DEVILMENT IS THIS?"

"NO, SHE HAS A FACE FOR A BOTTOM!"

Fanny cleared the train in seconds, which meant she had a whole carriage to herself. She **even** put her feet up on the seats. When the ticket inspector came round, he was so alarmed he jumped out of the window.

This was good news as Fanny had a super-saver ticket that was **only** valid off-peak on alternate Thursdays.

The first stop was the Royal Opera House. The mighty opera SUPERSTAR Luigi Lasagnotti, who weighed as much as a small car, was on the stage. Luigi was giving his Don Giovanni, and the audience of well-to-do lords,

ladies and gentlemen were **pretending** to enjoy it. Fanny crept in through the stage door. When Luigi was hitting a particularly low note (around the same frequency as a gorilla's burp)...

"OOOOOOOOOOOOOOOOOOOOOOOOOOOOOH!"

...Fanny burst on to the stage. Luigi was so
shocked at the sight of this little girl who appeared to
have a bottom for a face that his low note
became a high note.

"OOOAAAAEEEEIIIIIIIIIIIIIIIIII!"

The sound was so **shrill** and piercing that the audience members had to cover their ears.

They pelted poor Luigi with **rotten fruit,** as was the tradition when an **OPERA STAR** hit the wrong note. *"ARGH!"*

Fanny hid behind him, using the man as a human shield. Signor Lasagnotti was a big eater, and tried to catch as much of the fruit as he could in his mouth. However, there were so many pieces of fruit that he couldn't catch everything, and was soon standing there soaked to the skin. As he burst into tears...

"BOO HOO HOO! MAMMA MIA!"

...Fanny made her escape.

The next stop was **10 Downing Street,** home to the prime minister. A policeman was standing guard outside the **famous** black door. At his feet was Larry, the famous Downing Street cat (famous in feline circles). Larry saw Fanny approach first. The cat had seen some terrifying sights over the years:

A president of the United States with a face so orange he could be mistaken for one...

An Italian prime minister wearing a toupee so outrageous it looked like a squirrel that had been flattened by a truck was stuck to his head...

A Russian leader whose nose was so **big** and red from drinking **vodka** that he looked like the patient in the game Operation...

However, Fanny's funny face was the most startling thing Larry had **ever** seen. **"MIAOW!"** the cat screamed in terror. Larry leaped on top of the policeman's helmet, his cat bottom sticking right in the policeman's face.

The man couldn't see a thing.

"GET OFF ME! I will place you under arrest!" he said to the animal. "Don't make me fetch the little cat pawcuffs!"

As soon as he'd pulled the animal off, he was confronted with a sight **far worse** than a cat's bottom.

"ARGH!" he screamed, before placing the cat back on his head. The policeman banged on the big black door. "HELP! LET ME IN!"

The prime minister opened it. "What on earth is all this commotion?" she demanded. On seeing Fanny's funny face, she SCREAMED... "ARGH!"

...and slammed the big black door. She **slammed** it **so hard** that she *shattered* all the windows in 10 Downing Street.

SMASH!

CRACK!

"Arrest that bottom-faced girl!" bellowed the prime minister, but with the cat still perched on his head the policeman couldn't see a thing. By mistake, he handcuffed the prime minister.

All the press photographers waiting outside began taking pictures, and the image of the prime minister being led away in **handcuffs** by a policeman with a cat on his head was seen on **every** newspaper front page around the **world**.

The prime minister felt **SO** ashamed that she wrote to herself asking for her resignation, which she accepted.

Dear Prime Minister,
It is with great regret and huge personal sadness that I write to you or you write to me – I am confused – offering my/your resignation.

Yours sincerely,
Prime Minister

Dear Prime Minister,
It is with great regret and huge blah blah blah that I/you accept your/my resignation.

Yours sincerely,
Prime Minister

Finally, Fanny arrived at her last stop, Buckingham Palace. Giving Her Majesty the Queen a **big fat** fright would be the ultimate thrill for Fanny.

There was some building work taking place in the courtyard. A new surface was being laid down, and there were builders and cement mixers **everywhere.** Two of the Queen's Guard stood outside, protecting the royal family.

These soldiers were famous for standing to attention for **hours on end**, staring straight ahead in their tall bearskin hats. Nothing and nobody could distract them, though that was all about to change. One look at Fanny's face and the first guard shrieked and leaped into the arms of the other.

"ARGH!" Then the second guard BURST into tears...

"I WANT MY MUMMY!"

...and ran off down the road carrying the first in his arms, knocking over a fair few American tourists on the way.

"That **must** be the 'changing of the guard'," said one round lady with a Texan drawl.

"How quaint!" replied another.

"Now let's buy some fudge," said a third as they picked themselves up from the ground.

High up in Buckingham Palace, a window opened. An elderly lady in a dressing gown and curlers leaned out and bawled,

"WHAT'S ALL THIS BLASTED **NOISE?"**

Looking up, Fanny realised it was Her Majesty the Queen. That room must be the Queen's bedroom.

Fanny hid in the sentry box until the window was closed again. Then she stole a ladder from the builders, and climbed **all** the way up to that particular window, high on the top floor.

Peering through it, Fanny could see that the Queen was enjoying some afternoon tea. There were tea and scones, and a cake stand piled high with all kinds of delights that she was feeding to her corgis. Fanny tapped on the glass to get the Queen's attention and then quickly ducked out of view. The little girl waited until she heard the window slide open again before she bobbed up, showing off her **bottom face** in all its glory.

The Queen was SO **startled** she spat her tea right in Fanny's face.

"SPLURT!"

The force of the spray was so strong that it actually made the girl fall

backwards.

Fanny clung on to the ladder, but it toppled backwards too. She found herself heading straight towards the wet cement below.

"ARGH!"

the girl screamed in terror, finally feeling as frightened as all her victims.

Fanny landed in the cement with a giant

SPLAT!

The builders tried to save her, but the cement hardened in moments, and before they could pull her out she had become encased in it.

Fanny was rushed to hospital, but there was **no** hope for her. Her father agreed she should remain a statue as a warning to any naughty children who might follow in Fanny's footsteps.

The Queen rather liked the statue, and had it placed on a plinth next to her lions in Trafalgar Square. So, if you pass by the centre of London, do go and see the statue of the **bottom-faced** girl. Her father was right: her face really **did** become stuck like that. Forever.

THE
BOTTOM-FACED
GIRL

HANK'S
Pranks

Pranks CAN BE harmless. Pranks can be fun.

Not Hank's pranks.

Oh no.

They were deadly, as you might well expect from one of the world's worst children.

Not a day went by without Hank playing a **trick** on someone. It could be something simple like:

Deflating a **balloon** every time his teacher sat down to make it sound as if they'd **BLOWN OFF**...

Sticking strips of sticky tape to the doorframe so anyone passing through became s**tuck** in it...

Putting clingfilm round the toilet bowl so you *splashed* yourself as you peed...

Smearing butter all over the kitchen floor so it became

as **slippery** as an ice rink...

Tickling his sleeping father on the nose with a feather so he woke up with a giant **SNEEZE**...

Or something more elaborate like:

Pretending to be **poisoned** in the school cafeteria by
painting his face purple and then
lying on the floor, moaning loudly...

"URGH!
BEWARE THE **FISH PIE!"**

On a school trip to a history museum,
wrapping himself in toilet paper and
pretending to be one of the Egyptian
MUMMIES come to life!

"WHA HA!"

Concealing his arm up his
jumper, and then squirting ketchup all over
the woodwork room, pretending he had
sawn it off...

"NOOOO!"

Every time one of Hank's pranks landed, he would shout at the top of his voice, **"GOTCHA!"**

Hank's family was the main target of his pranks:

At his grandmother's house, he replaced her night cream with the real cream from the fridge. This meant she spent the whole night fighting off her six cats, who all tried to lick it off. **" M I A O W ! "**

"OFF!" yelled the poor old lady.

"GOTCHA!" said Hank.

His sister Molly had a terrible fear of sharks after seeing them on television, so when she went for her weekly swimming lesson Hank saw the perfect opportunity to terrorise her. He made a shark costume out of bin liners, fashioned a fin from a float then swam towards her.

"ARGH!" she screamed.

Now the girl is so frightened of water she won't even get in the bath.

"GOTCHA!" said Hank.

His father was allergic to **cheese**. Whenever
he had it, the man had to dash to the toilet
clutching his bottom for fear it might explode.
So Hank bought a huge slab of cheese, and cut it into
the shapes of biscuits. He then dipped the cheese
shapes in melted chocolate.

"Here you go, Dad, some lovely chocolate biscuits."

"Ah, thank you, Hank. What a good boy you are," said
Father. He took a large bite. Immediately he could
hear his tummy *FIZZING* and *POPPING*.

Before long he was clutching his
bottom and running for the toilet.

BLURT! **"GERONIMO!"**
yelled Father as he ran.

"GOTCHA!" said Hank.

The man's bottom hit the
toilet seat just as his bottom
exploded.

It was a dead heat.

Father didn't come out of there
for three whole days.

Hank's grandfather loved his nice comfy **slippers,** and kept them by his bed so he could slip into them first thing in the morning. Hank being Hank, he attached **roller-skates** to the bottom of each one. So when Grandpa slipped his slippers on he went fl^{y}in^{g} across his bedroom...

"WOOO!"

...only stopping when he hit the wardrobe.

CLUNK!

"GOTCHA!"
said Hank.

His uncle and aunt fared
no better. Uncle Tony's hobby
was collecting prized remote-
controlled planes, whereas Auntie Katy's
hobby was looking after her gerbils. Hank
had the idea of combining their two
hobbies. While he was staying over at
their house, he put the gerbils in the
planes and took them to the skies.

BRUM!

The poor creatures were so
petrified they parachuted out.

"EEEEEEEEEEEE!"

The sky was littered with the little
creatures floating to the ground.

"GOTCHA!
GOTCHA!
GOTCHA!"

shouted Hank.

The person who Hank managed to upset most with his pranks was his own mother. The poor lady was always incredibly jumpy. You would be too if your son played devilish tricks on you EVERY **SINGLE** DAY.

Now, all sorts of things could set Mother's nerves off:

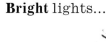 The doorbell **ringing**...

Little **yappy** dogs...

Someone **dropping** a spoon...

Bright lights...

The **dark**...

The *beep, beep, beep* of a lorry reversing...

A **sneeze**...

The sound of flip-flops **flip-flopping**...

The noise of a bubblegum bubble **popping**...

Loud, **dramatic** music at the start of the news...

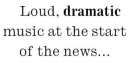

Someone **playing** the castanets...

Needless to say, Mother hated having tricks played on her. Her son showed **no mercy**. It was because her reaction to his pranks was the greatest that Hank dreamed up devilish tricks to play on her.

The boy would think of the next day's pranks while enjoying his nightly bath. Mother always moaned that he spent **far** too much time in there. Every evening after her son had been in the bath for over an hour, she would pound on the bathroom door.

BUNG! BUNG! BUNG!

"Hank, come out! If you stay in that bath a second longer, my boy, you will end up withered like a **prune!**" Mother would shout.

"'Ow dare you!" Hank would bawl back from the bath. "Never interrupt a genius at work!"

"What do you mean 'at work'?" the lady would splutter. "You are not at work – you are in the bath!"

"I AM FINKING!"

As usual, it was while lying in the bath that Hank had what he thought was a genius idea.

DING!

"This is the prank to end all pranks!" he proclaimed as he rubbed his stumpy hands together in glee. "This will be my masterpiece. Shakespeare 'ad '*Amlet*, Leonardo da Vinci 'ad the statue of *Dave Somebody*, Mozart 'ad… some music fing or some'ink. Well, this is mine!"

Hank thought he could give his mother the shock of her life if he pretended he had been in the bath all night.

No doubt this would cause her to go bananas.

STEAM would come out of her **ears**...

She would go **cross-eyed**...

Her **hair** would stand **up** on end...

She would **SLAP** herself in the **face**...

She would start **hopping** on one **leg**...

She would **bang** herself on the **head** with a tambourine...

Her **face** would turn purple...

She would pass out and fall to the **floor** with a **CLONK!**

Ideally for Hank, **all** of the above.

So, on the morning our story begins, Hank got out of bed super **early.** This isn't something the world's worst children often do, unless they have an **evil plan**, and Hank definitely had one of those.

First, he slipped out of his pyjamas, and put on his swimming trunks and goggles. Next, Hank found his box of **pens**, tiptoed out of his bedroom and sneaked downstairs to the kitchen. There he emptied the freezer of all the ice cubes, which he carried in a bucket up to the bathroom. Once safely inside, Hank closed the door behind him as quietly as he could. **CLICK!**

Now Hank looked at himself in the bathroom mirror. How could he make it look as if he'd been in the bath all night? He took out a brown felt-tip pen, and drew **hundreds** of lines all over his face and body. In no time at all, the boy looked exactly like an unusually large prune.

SPOT THE DIFFERENCE

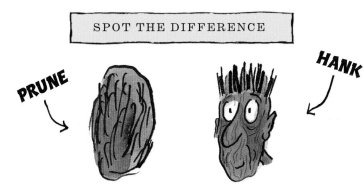

PRUNE

HANK

As silently as possible, Hank ran the **cold** tap, and added all the **ice**. If the bath was hot, nobody would believe that he'd been in there all night. With trepidation, Hank stepped into the bath.

"BRRR!"

It was cold!

Last, he lay down in the water and waited for his mother to wake up. Sure enough, after a short while, Hank heard the sound of his mother **clomping** down the corridor to the bathroom.

CLOMP! **CLOMP!** CLOMP!

YES! thought Hank, though he kept **quiet** so as not to spoil the awful **surprise.** What a shock was awaiting his mother! It was sure to make her go absolutely **GAGA!**

Except Mother never looked into the bath. The lady had only just got up, and was still **half asleep.**

She slumped down on the toilet for a few moments before flushing the **chain**.

FLUSH!

Mother was out of the bathroom in moments.

Oh dear, thought Hank. *Still, she is bound to come back soon, and then* **GOTCHA!**

Now it was beginning to feel horribly **c-c-cold** in the bath. Hank started *sh~sh~shivering* and his teeth began ch-ch-chattering.

CHATTER! CHATTER! CHATTER!

What's more, the boy could feel his skin was puckering and withering like that of a prune. There had been no need for the felt-tip lines, after all. Still, Hank had come this far – he couldn't give up now! Mother was sure to return to the bathroom any moment.

Moments came and moments went.

After what seemed like an hour, Mother did **finally** return to the bathroom. But, instead of turning on the shower and seeing her son lying in the bath, the lady washed her face in the basin. Her daughter, Molly, breezed past her to grab her toothbrush.

"Have you seen Hank?" asked Mother.

"He must still be in bed," replied the girl.

"Oh! Let the little devil sleep, then! The more time he spends in bed, the less time he has to play his nasty **tricks** on us!"

Soon the pair left the bathroom. Hank was feeling like a bit of a fool, a freezing-cold fool, as he lay in wait in his bath, which felt colder than swimming in the Arctic.

Eventually, the boy's father came into the bathroom. Surely **he** would spot Hank? The man began to wash under his arms with a flannel. Hank tried to cry out, **"LOOK IN THE BATH!"** but by now he was too **cold** to speak as his mouth had **FROZEN SOLID**.

When his father left the bathroom, Hank realised that he would have to stop the prank on his mother. He could hear the family downstairs in the kitchen having breakfast.

Climbing out of the bath was quite a task for Hank, because his whole body was **shaking**.

The boy checked his reflection in the mirror.

He had turned

bright blue.

Feeling as if he'd been encased in **ICE**, he shuffled stiffly across the corridor to the top of the stairs. Hank's legs were frozen solid.

As he tried to take a step, he fell forward and

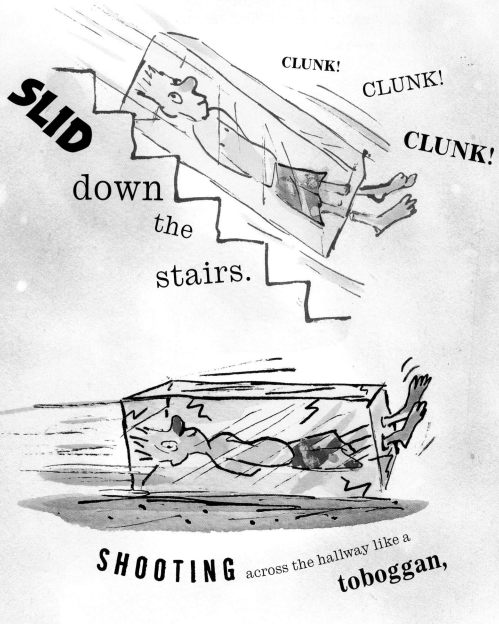

CLUNK!

CLUNK!

CLUNK!

SLID

down

the

stairs.

SHOOTING across the hallway like a **toboggan,**

Hank's head SLAMMED into the kitchen door

and he came to

a **halt**

just at

Mother's **feet.**

The lady looked down at her blue son.

"What on earth?" she proclaimed.

"It's just another of his pranks!" said

Molly, who was munching on a piece

of toast.

"Oh yes!" said Father, barely looking up from his morning newspaper.

"He's all wet and, look, he's drawn **lines** all over himself with a felt-tip pen!" exclaimed Molly. "And he must have painted himself blue. Hank has really **outdone** himself this time!"

"He looks like a Smurf!" observed Father.

"What's it all about?" asked the lady, puzzled.

Molly thought for a moment, and looked down at her brother as he lay **shivering** on the lino.

"Hank's trying to make it look like he's been in the bath **all night!**"

"Oh yes!" exclaimed Mother.

All three burst out **laughing**.

"HA! HA! HA!"

"The joke's on **you** this time, Hank!" said Father.

"I love it!" added Mother, her eyes lit up with glee that the tables had finally been turned.

Still Hank lay **shivering** on the floor.

"H-H-H-H-H-E-E-E-E-E-L-L-L-L-P-P-P-P-P!"

he chattered.

The three roared with laughter.

"HA! HA! HA!"

"GOTCHA!"

they all shouted in unison, before returning to their breakfast. *MUNCH! SLURP! RUSTLE!*

After Hank had been lying there on the kitchen floor for a good few hours, unable to speak or move, the family finally suspected that something might be **really** wrong.

The boy was rushed to hospital in an ambulance.

NEE-NAW! *NEE-NAW!* *NEE-NAW!*

The doctors and nurses raced his stretcher into the children's ward and wedged him up against the radiator.

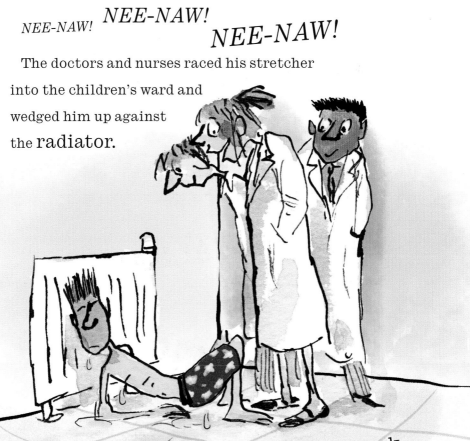

It took Hank a whole week to **thaw out.**

Embarrassingly, the boy needed an operation to remove his swimming trunks. Because of the extreme cold, they'd become welded to his bottom.

That's what can happen when a prank goes terribly wrong. If you play a trick on someone, the joke can end up being on you.

GOTCHA!

HONEY
the Hogger

HONEY **hogged** THE bathroom. The girl would spend SO long getting ready that by the time she left the house whatever she was going to had long since finished. Often days before.

HONEY THE HOGGER

The reason that Honey was such a **hogger** was that she had the longest beauty regime in the history of the world. It was even longer than Cleopatra's, and she bathed in **ass's milk.**

It was even longer than Elizabeth I's, who had leeches attached to her body for hours to feast on her blood so she could look pale. It was even longer than Marie Antoinette's, and she had a pouf of hair a metre tall that needed teasing every morning.

No, Honey Flunk's beauty regime was epic.

First, the girl would use a **mud mask** on her face, for which she stole her brother Horace's modelling clay.

Next, she would do her own hair extensions by gluing **spaghetti** to the strands of her hair.

Third, she would work on her tan using **gravy** granules. These she would mix with hot water and rub all over her skin until it was a deep shade of tan. That is why Honey, despite her name, always smelled a bit beefy.

Then it was time to go to battle with her **nasal** hair. This Honey would strip out with sticky tape. She would then put the sticky tape back in the drawer for the next person to use, complete with a selection of her **nasal** hair.

A cooling eye mask followed. This was achieved by sticking two **ice-cream** cones on to her eyes.

Finally, Honey would smooth down her eyebrows, using her brother's hamster as a brush.

Needless to say, her beauty regime was so BONKERS that Honey always ended up looking far **worse** than when she'd started.

BEFORE

AFTER

The problem for the rest of her family was that Honey would **hog** the bathroom for so long that they could never use it. There was only **one** toilet in the house, and her brother Horace was one of those boys who needed to *pee* every five minutes. Absolutely anything could set him off. It could be:

THE SOUND OF A DRIPPING RADIATOR...
TURNING ON A TAP...
GOING OVER A SPEED BUMP...
LOOKING AT A POND...
WHALE SONG...
DIPPING HIS TOE IN A PADDLING POOL...
SOMEONE COMING UP BEHIND HIM AND SHOUTING, **"Boo!"**

THE SOUND OF RAIN HITTING A TENT...
SITTING ON A WASHING MACHINE DURING ITS WASH CYCLE...
COLD WEATHER...
WARM WEATHER...

LOOKING AT A PICTURE OF THE NIAGARA FALLS...
GOING PAST A RESERVOIR ON A BUS...
THINKING ABOUT ANYTHING YELLOW, SUCH AS BANANAS, RUBBER DUCKS AND NEW YORK TAXI CABS...

Often, Horace would be caught short while his sister was **hogging** the bathroom. The poor boy was forced to use all kinds of receptacles in an emergency. And it was always an emergency. He would use:

A goldfish bowl...

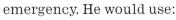

An **egg cup.** Actually several egg cups...

A plant pot... The plant promptly died. If flora and fauna could write letters, this plant would write an exceptionally **stern** one:

To Whom It May Concern,

The most unspeakable thing has happened, so unspeakable, in fact, that I cannot speak of it. The result is I have died, which I have to tell you I am not happy about. Not one bit.

Yours sincerely,

A crocus

PS I am a plant.
PPS I am dead.

Being a **big** sister, Honey liked to **tease** her little brother. Knowing he was always being caught short, she set about making his life a **misery.** Honey was one of the world's **worst** children, after all. When he desperately needed to go, she would make matters **worse** for him. When Horace was outside, banging on the bathroom door...

THUD! THUD! THUD!

...Honey would **run** the taps.

P S S S S T !

The sound of running water was enough to make Horace cross his legs and hop up and down on the spot.

"I NEED TO GO!"

he would shout.

HOP! HOP! HOP!

"Hee! Hee! Hee!" she would snicker.

Or while he was sleeping soundly...

"zzzz! ZZZZ! ZZZZ!"

...Honey would place the boy's fingers in a cup of warm water. This would make Horace wake up with the most desperate urge to **run** to the toilet.

"ARGH! I REALLY NEED TO GO!"

He would be so desperate he wouldn't even turn on the lights and would mistake the wardrobe for the bathroom.

"That's better!" he would sigh in relief.

"Hee! Hee! Hee!" Honey would snigger as she heard the confusion.

On the particular night our story unfolds, Honey devised a **devilishly cruel** plan for her little brother. A plan that would leave the boy absolutely **B U R S T I N G** for a *pee*.

First, Honey poured hot, hot chilli powder on to Horace's dinner.

When he tasted just one spoonful of mashed potato, he spat it right across the room.

"EURGH!" S P L U R T! **SPLAT!**

It hit the window. **TING!**

"HELP!" he cried.

Of course, Horace had no idea why his eyes were running, his face had turned bright **red** and his tongue felt like it was on **fire.**

"What on earth is the matter, dearest brother, whom I love beyond compare?" lied Honey.

"I don't know!" cried Horace. "I feel like I am burning up!"

"Poor, poor you. However could this have happened?"

"PLEASE! HELP!"

"WATER! YOU NEED WATER!" Honey exclaimed. A wicked grin spread across her gravy-coloured face.

"QUICKLY! PLEASE!" he yelled. His face was now redder than a tomato.

Here is a helpful graph of red things:

WATERMELON · POSTBOX · LOBSTER · LONDON BUS · RUBY · CHILLI · LITTLE RED RIDING HOOD'S CAPE · SNOOKER BALL · FIRE EXTINGUISHER · CHINESE FLAG · FERRARI · TOMATO · HORACE'S FACE

QUITE RED

VERY RED

The girl yanked her little brother by the arm and pulled him into the kitchen.

"This way, my darling sibling!" she said.

In the kitchen cupboard she found the tallest glass, and filled it to the brim with water from the tap.

"DRINK! DRINK!" she ordered.

Honey lifted the glass up to his mouth, and poured the **whole lot** down Horace's throat.

GUZZLE! GUZZLE! **GULP!**

As soon as he had finished it, Honey announced, "You are still **very** red, my darling Horace. Another!"

Once again, she poured a glass **full** of water down his throat.

GUZZLE! GUZZLE! GUZZLE! **GULP!**

And **another.**

GUZZLE! GUZZLE! GUZZLE! GUZZLE! **GULP!**

And **another.**

GUZZLE! GUZZLE! GUZZLE! GUZZLE!

GUZZLE! **GULP!**

And **another.**

GUZZLE! GUZZLE! GUZZLE!

G<small>UZZLE</small>! G<small>UZZLE</small>! **GULP!**

And **another.**

G<small>UZZLE</small>! G<small>UZZLE</small>! <small>GUZZLE</small>! G<small>UZZLE</small>! <small>GUZZLE</small>!
<small>GUZZLE</small>! G<small>UZZLE</small>! <small>GUZZLE</small>! **GULP!**

And, just to make **sure** her **wicked** plan would work, she poured one last glass of water down her little brother's gullet.

"Thank you!" said Horace. The boy's face had now gone back to normal and he didn't feel as if he were sitting in an **oven** any more. However, a new problem had arisen. Now he had gallons upon gallons of water sloshing around inside him. Enough to fill a **paddling pool**. He felt like a **GIANT** water balloon, and looked like one too.

SPOT THE DIFFERENCE

HORACE

GIANT WATER BALLOON

Needless to say, Horace was absolutely **BURSTING** for a *pee*.

"I NEED TO GO!" he shouted, **biting** on his lip to try and hold it in. **"OUCH!"**

"Oh, I just **need** to use the bathroom to comb my hair first, Horace," said Honey with a smirk.

"NO! PLEASE! I NEED TO GO! LIKE, NOW!"

"Where are your manners, little brother?" replied the girl. "Ladies first!" she said, and rushed ahead to get to the bathroom before him.

"**NO!** PLEASE! I REALLY NEED TO GO! LIKE, RIGHT NOW! LIKE, ACTUALLY, LIKE, A MOMENT AGO!"

Honey elbowed her now-voluminous brother out of the way, and slammed the bathroom door behind her. **BANG!**

Then she locked it. **CLICK!**

Horace was so desperate to go that the boy did **everything** he could to stop the flow. He crossed his waterlogged legs, hopped on the spot and began pounding on the bathroom door.

BANG! **BANG! BANG!**

SLOSH SLOSH SLOSH! he sloshed.

"HONEY! LET ME IN!

PLLLEEEEEEAAASSSE!"

"Come back in a few hours, sweet Horace," cooed the girl from the other side of the locked door. **"Hee! Hee! Hee!"** she snickered to herself. A wicked grin spread across her face. Honey was enjoying this immensely.

Horace didn't have a few hours. He didn't have a few minutes. The boy barely had a few **seconds.** Horace charged around the house looking for somewhere, anywhere, to go. The gallons of liquid **slished** and **sloshed** and **slushed** and **slashed** around inside him. If only he could have a *pee-pee!*

BUT WHERE?

Not in the plant pot! He would be in big trouble if he massacred another plant.

Not in the goldfish bowl! The goldfish had forgiven him once – he was unlikely to again!

Horace raced to the window. This was the **perfect** solution. He could go out of the window! shaking with anticipation, he opened it.

Horace could already feel a sense of great relief.

But before he *peed* the boy looked down.

DISASTER!

On the lawn below, next-door's cat Pusskin was preening herself.

"OH NO!" cursed Horace. "I'll **never** go to heaven if I *pee* on a cat!"

The boy guessed right. There are a number of things so awful that if you did them you would never, ever, ever go to heaven. These include:

Blowing your nose on a curtain...

Putting a cactus in your father's underpants...

Scoffing all of Granny's toffees when she dozes off in front of the TV...

Bursting a toddler's toy balloon...

Eating a curry on public transport...

Letting off a BANGER in a library...

Coughing on a gerbil...

Not flushing the toilet when you have done a number two the size of a submarine...

Taking a bite out of every cake in a cake shop then running off without paying...

Wiping a bogey on a puppy...

The poor boy bit on his finger to hold the tidal wave in.

"OW!" It hurt.

That was **no** use. He had to find somewhere, anywhere to go. In desperation Horace hopped back to the bathroom door and thumped on it as **hard** as he possibly could.

BOOM! BOOM! BOOM!

"I won't be **too** long, my dear Horace! I am just detangling the tiniest tangle in my hair. Why not come back first thing tomorrow morning?" called back Honey. "HEE! HEE! HEE!"

"I CAN'T WAIT ANY LONGER!" yelled the boy. Having bitten his lip and his finger, he turned his attention to a water pipe on the wall and bit straight through it.

CRUNCH!

Now the water pipe had a **large** mouth-sized hole in it.

"Oops!" he said.

But at that exact moment Horace had the most **splendiferous** idea. He could *pee* into the broken pipe! That is **exactly** what he did.

"AAH!" the boy sighed, and the water began gushing out of him.

Honey pressed her ear to the bathroom door. What was happening? This **wasn't** the plan! She wanted her little brother to suffer!

Distracted by what was occurring on the other side of the door, Honey didn't notice what was going on in the bathroom. The pipe must have been connected to the **toilet** because now the bowl was **overflowing** with water.

GLUG! GLUG! GLUG!

In no time, the bathroom was becoming a swimming pool.

Honey noticed her feet were **wet**, then her knees, then her waist.

That's funny, she thought.

The girl turned round to see that **water** was gushing out of the bowl, and in moments the bathroom was now **completely** underwater.

"**NOooo!**" she blubbed.

Desperately, Honey swam over to the toilet to make the water **stop.** She dived down to the flush and pressed it.

FLUSH!

Honey smiled as all the water in the bathroom began swirling down the bend. But in an instant she found herself swirling down the bend too!

"ARGH!" she yelled.

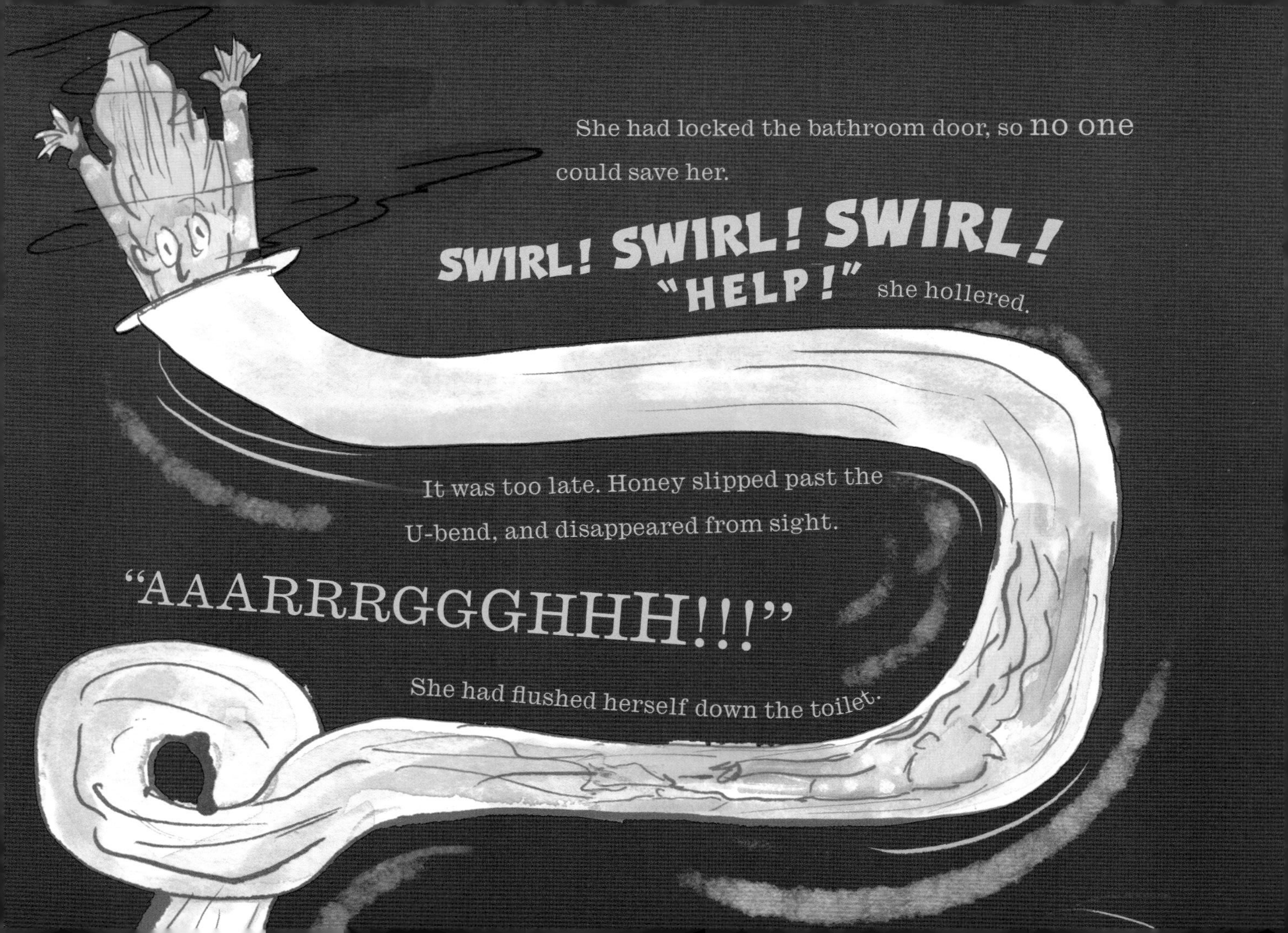

She had locked the bathroom door, so no one could save her.

SWIRL! SWIRL! SWIRL! SWIRL!

"**HELP!**" she hollered.

It was too late. Honey slipped past the U-bend, and disappeared from sight.

"**AAARRRGGGHHH!!!**"

She had flushed herself down the toilet.

The girl was **sucked** and **s q u e e z e d** down tube after tube before she was deposited down in the **sewer**.

"YUCKETY YUCK YUCK YUCK YUCK!"

her voice echoed in the gloom. But deep underground **no one could hear her.**

It was **impossible** for the girl to climb back up the tubes. They were far too slippery. So Honey became **trapped** in the sewers for **all eternity,** splattered from head to toe in dirt and **grime** and goodness knows what.

SPLAT!

Which is, **of course**, what can happen if you **hog** the bathroom.

As for Horace, you will be pleased to learn that he can now *pee* whenever his heart desires.

"HEE! HEE! HEE!"

Vain
VALENTINE

VALENTINE WAS HANDSOME, and boy did he know it! He was so vain he couldn't walk past a mirror without checking his reflection in it. One time, some boys at his school came into the toilets and caught Valentine kissing himself in the mirror.

Valentine believed that because he was *handsome* he should be famous too. He had **no** talents of any kind but, like a lot of famous people, he wasn't going to let that hold him back. The boy annoyed everyone by acting as if he were famous, strutting around the school wearing **sunglasses**. He never took them off, even when it was dark, and spent all day bumping into things as he couldn't see where he was going.

BOOF!

"Ouch!"

If a teacher handed him a detention slip, he would assume they were asking for his **autograph**, scribble on it and hand it back to them.

"Have that framed! Instant heirloom!"

Valentine would refuse to take part in sports in case a stray ball bashed into his perfect face.

"Sorry, guys! My *face* is my fortune! If I looked like you, I would be **broke!**"

Once, he developed a big red **spot** on the end of his nose, and was so horrified he didn't come into school for a whole term.

"NOOOOOOOOOO! I thought I was **FLAWLESS!** ABSOLUTELY **FLAWLESS!**"

Valentine didn't have time for friends. Instead he spent the whole of break-time and lunchtime taking **SELFIES**.

CLICK!

CLICK!

CLICK!

At last count, he had 895,731 pictures of himself on his phone. During any downtime, he would scroll through these, admiring **himself**.

"That's a great shot of **me**. Another great shot of **me**. Wow, yet another great shot of **me**. Why didn't anyone tell me I am SOOOOOO *handsome?*"

CLICK!

CLICK!

CLICK!

Valentine would claim that Valentine's Day was named after **him.** He would send hundreds of Valentine's cards to **himself,** which he would open during lessons to try to impress everybody.

"Oh no, this is **embarrassing!**

Yet another card professing undying *love*

for little old me!"

The girls in his school would **never** send him a card. He might have been *good-looking*, but his personality made him **repulsive.** Valentine really was one of the world's **worst** children.

One day, Valentine had what he thought was a brilliant idea. An idea he was sure would propel him to stardom, **SUPERSTARDOM** or even **MEGASTARDOM**. He would enter the record books by setting a new world record for the biggest game of *kiss chase* ever. Valentine would be the **only** boy, and there would be hundreds of girls pursuing him, desperate for a *kiss*. Just the thought of it made him smirk the smirkiest smirk that had ever been smirked.

But he couldn't do it alone, so Valentine put up hundreds of **posters** with his face on them all around the school.

What Valentine didn't know was that **none** of the girls in his school **wanted** to kiss him. In fact, they found his vanity **loathsome,** and he was a complete joke. The "PRETTY GIRLS ONLY, PLEASE" part made them loathe him even more.

The **smartest** pupil in the school was named Emmeline. As soon as she saw the posters go up, she spread word around the school that **all** the girls should meet in secret, as she had a **plan** that would teach this idiot boy a **lesson.**

GIRLS, THIS IS YOUR CHANCE OF A LIFETIME TO KISS THE HANDSOMEST BOY IN THE SCHOOL, IF NOT THE WORLD: VALENTINE. (OF COURSE.)

MEET ME IN THE SCHOOL PLAYGROU...

FRIDAY

The next morning, they all gathered in the sports hall before lessons began. Emmeline climbed on to a gym box so she could address the crowd.

"Sisters!"

she began. Emmeline had a slight lisp, which only made her sound brainier than she already was. "I am sure you have all seen the disgusting posters *vain* Valentine has put up all over the school?"

There was a chorus of "Yes" followed by some loud booing.

"BOO!"

"How dare he write 'PRETTY GIRLS ONLY'?! Every single one of us, no matter what we look like, is beautiful."

There was a huge cheer from the crowd.

"HOORAY!"

"And we must teach this revolting creature a lesson!"

"YES!" went the crowd.

"But how?" asked a girl at the back, named Sylvia.

"He wants a *kiss chase.* So let's give him a *kiss chase.*"

The girls looked at each other and began to murmur. How would that teach Valentine a lesson?

Emmeline smiled. She knew what was coming.

"Let's chase him all the way **out** of this school!"

"YES!" The girls broke out into wild applause.

"With any luck, he might never come back!"

Emmeline expounded upon her **plan**, and swore all the girls to secrecy.

On Friday afternoon, just before four o'clock, Valentine made his way to the playground. There he met with the official from the world-records book. She was a stern-looking woman, dressed in a blazer and skirt, holding a clipboard. Things got off to a *frosty* start.

"Hi, **babes!**" said Valentine, bounding up to her. He lifted his dark glasses. "Yes, it's really me. Valentine *Glorious.*" Yes, that really **was** his surname.

"My name is Miss Pankhurst, Mr Glorious," replied the lady. "And I am certainly not your '**babe**'."

The boy was taken aback. In his head, every female on the planet adored him. "I said '**babes**' not '**babe**'."

"Well, that is not only patronising, but also grammatically incorrect. Now, where are all these girls for your world-record attempt? You can't do a *kiss chase* on your own!"

Valentine looked around the empty playground. "Don't worry, **babes**, I mean Miss Pankhurst. All the **chicks**…"

The lady gave the boy a filthy look. Valentine continued to dig himself deeper.

"I mean **honeys**, no... **dolls**... erm... **chicks?**"

"Why don't you just call them 'ladies', Mr Glorious?"

"Ladies? I had never thought of that. Yes, all right, then – MY ladies."

Miss Pankhurst shook her head as all the young ladies in the school **marched** on to the playground, led by Emmeline.

A smug smile spread across Valentine's face. This was his **dream.** Not only were hundreds of girls going to chase him for a *kiss* but he would enter the record books and become A STAR.

Valentine studied the crowd, and his smile turned to a scowl. "I did say pretty girls only!"

The girls all tutted their disapproval. What a truly **despicable** child he was.

Miss Pankhurst rolled her eyes and took over. "Right, ladies. If I could have you all standing **behind** that white line, please.

Thank you so much.

This is the world-record attempt for the largest-ever *kiss chase*. The current record holder is pop star Mr Brad Bratters, who was chased by three hundred and seventeen of his fans after his concert in Las Vegas. They chased Mr Bratters all the way to the Grand Canyon, where he plummeted to his death. Which was a **sad** day for Mr Bratters, if **not** the people of the world, who will not miss Mr Bratters's smug little face and annoying songs. Still, it is, up to this point, the world's largest recorded *kiss chase*. I have counted three hundred and forty-two young ladies here today, comfortably clear of the current record.

Mr Glorious, are you **ready?**"

"I think I have a hair out of place!" said Valentine, stroking his fingers across his head.

All the girls sighed and ROLLED their eyes. He rushed to a window and, examining his reflection, patted the one tiny strand of hair that was **not** slicked back perfectly with all the others. Next, he took the opportunity to smooth down his painstakingly **plucked** eyebrows.

Finally, he winked at himself, and smiled before saying, "It's such a shame I can't **marry myself.**"

Emmeline mimed throwing up, which greatly amused the other girls.

"Ha! **Ha!**" they laughed.

" S H U S H ! " hissed Emmeline, not wanting Valentine to know they had a secret **plan.**

"Right. I am ready, **baby,**" announced the boy.

Miss Pankhurst grimaced.

"**Ladies**, are you ready?"

"YES!" they all chimed in together. The girls of Valentine's school had been waiting for this for a long, long time.

Behind their backs they were all clasping **masks** they had made. Every single one was of Valentine. He had put so many posters of himself up around the school that it was easy for the girls to cut round his face and poke through two eye holes.

Emmeline gave the order. **"Masks on, sisters!"**

It was a startling sight: 342 girls all looking exactly like the boy they were about to chase.

Valentine took in the scene. It was FREAKY!

"W-w-what the...?" spluttered the boy.

But, before he could say whatever he was going to say next, Emmeline spoke up.

"You *love* **yourself** SO much, Valentine, that we thought you would like to be chased by your **own** stupid face!

Now, **CHARGE!**"

Her army of sisters all started running as if they were going into **BATTLE.**

"NOOOOOOOOO!"

screamed Valentine, and he started fleeing desperately across the playground. **"HELP!"** he cried.

But **none** came.

Instead, hundreds of feet came pounding towards him. He passed a puddle. Valentine couldn't resist stopping to check his reflection in it. Even though his face was **STREAMING** with tears and snot,

Valentine still commented on himself:

"*Perfection!*"

Unfortunately for Valentine, this stop to admire himself would prove to be his undoing. Together the girls of the school had the power of a herd of **STAMPEDING** wildebeest. Vain Valentine was trampled underfoot.

"STOP!" ordered Emmeline.

But it was too late.

The boy had been **FLATTENED** like a **pancake**.

The crowd parted. The girls took off their masks to look down at what they had done.

"Oh no," said Emmeline, full of sorrow. "I think we've **killed** him."

"Still, on the bright side, you have set a new **world record for the flattest boy ever,"** added Miss Pankhurst.

Silence descended upon the playground like thick **s n o w.**

"So I **am** going to be in the **world-record books!"** came a voice. "I am going to be even more **FAMOUS** than I already am, and I am already very **FAMOUS**."

It was **Valentine.**

The **FLATTENED** boy rose slowly to his feet.

He was now as tall and as wide as a house.

"That is **great** news!"

"Yes... yes..." replied Miss Pankhurst.

"I feel a bit *strange*," said Valentine.

"Do I **look** strange?"

"No, no, no," muttered everyone unconvincingly.

Like a sail, he wafted over to a classroom window to take a look at the reflection of himself.

His face now resembled a dinner plate. In the centre was a **squashed** nose, and his eyes were now a skip away from each other. Valentine studied himself for a moment. "Still **got it!**" he said.

All the girls looked on, open-mouthed in shock, as he billowed off.

"I hope for his sake there's not a gust of wind," remarked Emmeline, "or he might take off like a **kite.**"

"HA! HA! HA!"

they all laughed.

BONNIE
Bossypants

BOSSY FACE

BOSSY EVERYTHING

BOSSY THOUGHTS

BONNIE
Bossypants

BONNIE WAS THE **bossiest** girl who **ever** lived.
She would **boss** around all her classmates.

"Stop laughing like
that, Larissa. You sound
like a seal!"

PART
1

"Close your mouth when you are chewing, Cher! It makes you seem **awfully** common!"

"Lose the perm, Perri. You look like a poodle!"

She even **bossed** around all of her teachers.

"I know you are **extremely** old, Miss Drabble, but stop dribbling!"

"For goodness' sake, straighten your tie, Mr Trundle. You look like you slept in a ditch!"

"Learn how to pronounce your 'R's properly, Mr Richards! The animal you are referring to is a 'racoon' not a 'wacoon'! I have never heard of a 'WACOON'!"

And, of course, she **bossed** around her own family.

"Brother, don't play with your yo-yo at the table!"

"Father, stop picking your nose!"

"Mother, don't slurp when you **drink** your tea! It's DISGUSTING!"

The night our story begins, things came to a head at home. None of her family could bear Bonnie's **bossiness.** The four were sitting in icy silence round the dining table eating their supper. An already tense situation became unbearable when Bonnie's father didn't finish all the food on his plate.

"**Finish your peas,** Father, or you will be **forced** to eat them cold for breakfast!" ordered the girl.

"I am sorry, Bonnie," he began, "but I am stuffed. I couldn't eat another thing."

"I said **'finish them'!**" she repeated.

"Please don't make me! I think I will **burst!**"

"Then you will be forced to eat them cold for your breakfast!"

"NO!" replied Father.

"Not **cold** peas. PLEASE!

I hate cold peas.

They would make me

sick!"

"Eat your peas right **now** or I will stick one up each of your nostrils!"

Bonnie **wasn't** joking. She took two off her plate, ready to push them up her father's nose.

The timid little man burst into floods of tears.

"BOO HOO HOO!"

"Stop crying or I will fetch the bag of frozen peas out of the freezer and make you eat **every** last frost-covered one!"

This made the man cry even **LOUDER.**

"BOO HOO HOO!"

"Bonnie! Leave your father alone!" pleaded Mother.

"Did I tell you that you could talk? If you have something to say, Mother, put your hand in the air!"

"No, but—"

"I **said,** put your hand in the **air!"** growled the girl.

Reluctantly, Mother did so. Her daughter **made** the lady wait ages until letting her speak. In fact, Mother had to change arms as the first one grew too **tired.**

"Yes? Mother?"

"Thank you. Bonnie, I think I am speaking for **all** the family now. You have to **stop bossing** us around like this!"

Bonnie's eyes narrowed. "Right! Mother, Father, go to your room this instant!"

"But—" protested Mother.

"I said, this instant!"

The two grown-ups **sighed** and stood up from the table. They sloped off out of the dining room.

"Quickly, please!" Bonnie ordered.

"**Chop-chop!** Right, brother! Put that yo-yo down! You clear the table, and do **all** the washing-up and drying-up.

Do you understand me?"

Her little brother Benji nodded. The poor boy hadn't spoken a word since **birth.** Having the world's **bossiest** sister, it was easier to keep schtum.

Most of the time he spent curling and uncurling his yo-yo.

Upstairs in their bed, Mother and Father began talking. They had to whisper, because if they spoke too **loudly** they would get a **mighty** telling-off.

"Love?" hissed Father.

"Yes, my dear?" whispered Mother.

"What on earth are we going to do about Bonnie?"

"Mmm. Well, I've been thinking that this might be the **perfect** job for *WONDERNANNY.*"

"Who?" asked Father.

"WONDERNANNY! She is the STAR of her own television show called *WONDERNANNY* where she helps parents deal with the world's naughtiest children."

"Do you think she could deal with our Bonnie?"

"WONDERNANNY has **never** failed. Her catchphrase is

'Naughty children better watch out when **WONDERNANNY** is about!'"

"Then our Bonnie better **watch out!**" replied Father. Both giggled conspiratorially.

"Tee hee hee!"

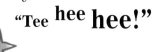

BOOM! BOOM! BOOM!

Someone was knocking on their bedroom door with all their might.

"YOU TWO! **STOP** TALKING IN THERE!" boomed Bonnie from the other side.

"Sorry!" the pair called out.

"SILENCE!" Bonnie ordered. And they were **silent.**

Moments later, they heard Bonnie scream. **"ARGH!** There's a spider in my bed."

Father went running into his daughter's bedroom wielding his slipper. He had to do this most nights as the girl **HATED** spiders, and, strangely, there was **always** one in the girl's bed. It was almost as if someone were putting them there.

The problem Father had was that, although he was running to rescue her, his daughter had just ordered him to be **silent.** As the man wasn't sure if he was allowed to speak yet, and did not want to incur her **wrath,** he used a pen and paper to communicate.

Please can I say something?

he scrawled, and showed it to Bonnie.

"YES!" the girl screamed. "Atrocious handwriting, though."

Thank you! he wrote.

"Where is the spider?" he asked.

"THERE! **KILL IT!**" said the girl, in quite a frenzy.

The man struggled to see it as it was so small. "It's only a baby one," he said.

"KILL IT!"

Father didn't have the heart to, so he whacked the bed right near the spider.

It bounced into the air on to the carpet.

PING!

"YOU MISSED!" she yelled. "Right, Mother, out of bed! I am sleeping in **your** bed tonight, and the two of you can sleep in here!"

Not for the first time, husband and wife SQUEEZED into their daughter's tiny single bed, while Bonnie sprawled out in their big double one.

The next morning, while Bonnie was at school **bossing** her teachers about as usual (she even gave the headmistress, Miss Clod, a detention for running in the corridor), Mother got to work. She found the telephone number for the producer of the TV show *WONDERNANNY.* Needless to say, he became terribly excited when told all about Bonnie's **bad** behaviour.

"No offence meant, but your daughter sounds fantastically awful!" he said.

"None taken," replied Mother.

"She **must** be one of the world's absolute worst children."

"I am **sorry** to say she is."

"Don't be sorry – she sounds like **TV GOLD!** Now, I just have some questions about Bonnie for you. *WONDERNANNY* always needs to know their likes, and even more importantly their dislikes. Here goes!

Question one: does your child have any phobias?"

"Oh yes. Spiders!"

"Terrific. Question two..."

Mother was shocked that there were quite so many questions, but she was sure it all must be important somehow.

Just as the conversation was wrapping up, Mother said, "We are at our wits' end. We can't live in the house with her any longer. Bonnie sets so many rules about this, that or the other it's like living in a **prison camp."**

"A prison camp! Ooh, you **must** say that on television!" squealed the producer excitedly.

"So please, please, can *WONDERNANNY* come as soon as possible?"

"Tomorrow! It's a Saturday, and that means we can film with your daughter all day."

"A day? Is that all you need?"

"Oh yes. Trust *WONDERNANNY!*

'Naughty children better watch out when *WONDERNANNY* is about!'

We have made hundreds of programmes over the years."

Indeed they **had.** Who could forget the episode

when *WONDERNANNY:*

CURED A BOY NAMED SOHUM OF HIS CHESS ADDICTION BY FORCING
HIM TO PLAY COMPUTER GAMES ALL DAY AND NIGHT INSTEAD.
"BUT I LOVE CHESS!" PROTESTED SOHUM.
"THEN YOU WILL LOVE NINJA WARRIORS OF ARMAGEDDON 7!"

CUT THE HEADPHONES CORD OF A GIRL CALLED ARIA WHO
LISTENED TO MUSIC ALL DAY AND INSTEAD FOLLOWED
HER AROUND SHOUTING IN HER EAR. "LA! LA! LA!"
"STOP!" PLEADED ARIA.

SNAPPED A GIRL NAMED GRACE'S RECORDER IN TWO
BECAUSE SHE PLAYED IT SO DREADFULLY.
"NOOOO! I NEED TO GIVE THE GIFT OF MY BEAUTIFUL
MUSIC TO THE PEOPLE OF THE WORLD!"
"IT WAS ENOUGH TO MAKE YOUR EARS BLEED!" SNAP!

STOPPED A BOY NAMED GEORGE'S OBSESSION
WITH WRESTLING STONE DEAD BY HURLING HIM
INTO A RING WITH A GARGANTUAN PROFESSIONAL
WRESTLER CALLED THE REFRIDGERATOR.
                                    "ARGH!"

MADE A GIRL NAMED LOTTIE STOP WOBBLING HER
WOBBLY TOOTH BY YANKING IT OUT WITH PLIERS.
"OUCH! THAT HURT!" LOTTIE CRIED.
"I KNOW. BUT I ENJOYED IT."

PUT A STOP TO A GIRL NAMED KAYA'S SHOPPING SPREES BY SETTING HER POCKET MONEY AT 1P PER HUNDRED YEARS.
"BUT I NEED NEW CLOTHES EVERY WEEK!"
"FROM NOW ON YOU CAN MAKE YOUR OWN CLOTHES FROM THESE OLD FLOWERY CURTAINS!"

CONTROLLED A GIRL NAMED KELLY'S FIERY TEMPERS BY DUNKING HER IN A FREEZING COLD LAKE TO COOL OFF.
"I'M C-C-C-C-COLD!"
"DON'T YOU WORRY. WHEN YOU ARE INSIDE THAT KILLER WHALE'S TUMMY, YOU SHOULD WARM UP!"

REPLACED A NAUGHTY CHILD NAMED LAYLA'S PONY WITH A DONKEY THAT WOULDN'T MOVE.
"GIDDY UP!"   "NEE-HAW!"

MADE A GIRL NAMED ISABEL BE ON TIME FOR ONCE BY WINDING BACK ALL THE CLOCKS IN THE HOUSE WHILE SHE SLEPT SO SHE ARRIVED TEN HOURS EARLY FOR EVERYTHING.
"WHERE IS EVERYBODY?"

STOPPED TWO WARRING TWINS NAMED KATIE AND MARCUS FROM FIGHTING BY DUMPING ONE IN THE ARCTIC AND ONE IN ANTARCTICA. SOMEHOW THEY STILL MANAGED TO THROW SNOWBALLS AT EACH OTHER. WHIZZ!   "OOF!"

"There has never, ever, EVER been a child that **WONDERNANNY** has not got the better of," concluded the producer.

"But you haven't met **my** daughter," sighed Mother.

"I know, and I can't wait. She sounds like an absolute **monster!** Bye-bye!"

Mother and Father didn't dare tell their daughter who was coming to the house **first thing** the next day.

At eight o'clock in the morning, on the dot, the doorbell rang, just as the producer had promised.

DING-DONG!

Mother, Father and little Benji all hid upstairs in a cupboard, so when Bonnie bellowed from her parents' bed...

"ANSWER THE **DOOR!**"

...no one did.

DING-DONG!

"I said, answer the door!"

The other three held their nerve.

DING-DONG!

"**RIGHT!** YOU THREE ARE ALL IN **BIG** TROUBLE! NONE OF YOU ARE GOING TO BE ABLE TO WATCH TV FOR A WEEK!" shouted the girl as she stomped down the stairs to the front door.

When Bonnie opened it, much to her surprise, TV's **WONDERNANNY** was standing right in front of her.

"Good morning!" sneered **WONDERNANNY**. She was a plump woman with glasses, and she wore her hair up in a NO-NONSENSE bun. Behind her was the producer holding a clipboard, a cameraman holding a camera and a sound-recordist holding what looked like a **cat** on a stick, a sort of **cat lolly,** but which was actually a microphone.

"*Naughty children better watch out when* **WONDERNANNY** *is about!*"

It wasn't a great catchphrase, but she was **sticking** to it.

"WONDERNANNY?" asked Bonnie. The girl was incredulous. She was on the back foot for once.

"Yes! It's your unlucky day!" **p u r r e d** the lady.

Bossy Bonnie looked aghast. Now she was going to be bossed about like she had never been bossed about before!

PART 2

"No, no, no!" protested Bonnie as **WONDERNANNY** stood on her doorstep. "There's been a terrible mix-up, **WONDERNANNY.** You **must** be here to see my little brother Benji. He never stops talking. You really need to have him taken away and locked in a **cage.**"

"Ha ha ha!" the TV star chuckled to herself, though it was one of those chuckles that sounded as if the person didn't actually find it funny. "I am not here to see him. I hear he is a delight. Silent, as all children should be. I am here to see..." **WONDERNANNY** left a dramatic pause. "...YOU!"

"Me?" Bonnie's voice went up. She couldn't hide her **shock**.

"Yes! You!" said the lady with a smirk. She smiled, and looked like a snake baring its **fangs,** ready to go in for the **kill.**

"Why me?" demanded the girl, sounding very hard done by.

"Because you, Bonnie Bonnington, are a complete and utter **bossypants!**"

The girl's face **soured.** It was as if she were chewing on a number of **wasps.** "You are the **bossypants,** so-called **WONDERNANNY!** Pah! Why don't you take your big, wobbly bottom and wibble-wobble off?"

WONDERNANNY smiled to herself, knowing the viewing figures for this episode were sure to hit the billions. This girl was beyond bad. She was the **absolute** worst of the worst.

"Because I am **not** going to," snapped the lady, and she pushed past the girl and made her way into the house. By this time, the family had gathered at the top of the stairs, eager to see what was going on.

"YOU DID THIS?" Bonnie turned to them and demanded. She looked and sounded like an **ogre.**

OGRE

BONNIE

"It **wasn't** my idea!" **spluttered** a frightened Father. "It was all your **mother's!**"

It took him less than a second to point the finger of blame.

"B-b-but, Bonnie, **please** forgive me. I thought it would be for the best," said Mother, trembling with **fear.**

"Mother! Get **down** here this instant!" ordered Bonnie. "I want you to clean the toilet with a **toothbrush!**"

"Mrs Bonnington, stay **UP** there!" ordered

WONDERNANNY.

"Come straight **down,** Mother!" demanded the girl.

Poor Mother looked mightily confused. Now she was being **bossed** around by **two** people at once.

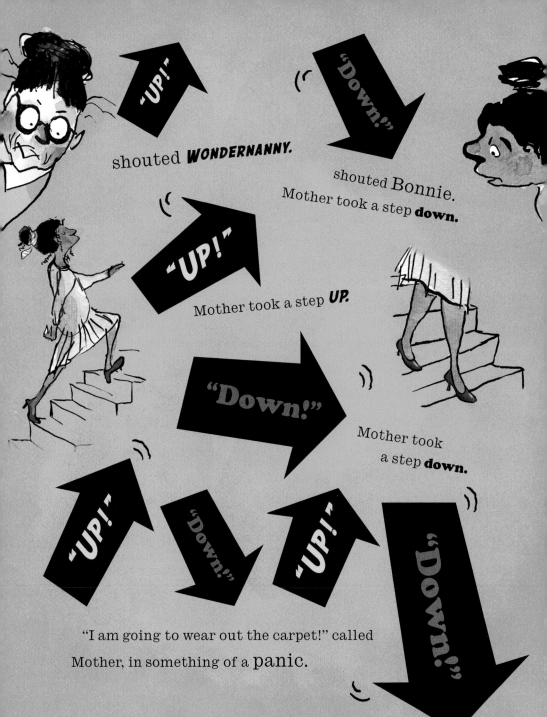

"UP!"

shouted **WONDERNANNY.**

"Down."

shouted Bonnie.
Mother took a step **down.**

"UP!"

Mother took a step **UP.**

"Down!"

Mother took
a step **down.**

"UP!"

"Down!"

"UP!"

"Down!"

"I am going to wear out the carpet!" called
Mother, in something of a panic.

"I am very disappointed in you, Mrs Bonnington," began **WONDERNANNY.**

"I know. I know," muttered Mother. "I am a terrible mother. I might as well go and jump in a lake!"

"There is **no** time for that, Mrs Bonnington!" snapped **WONDERNANNY.** "When your daughter bosses you around like this, you need to take charge, and **boss** her back!"

"But how?" pleaded Mother.

"Let's say this third step from the bottom here is the **NAUGHTY STEP!** When Bonnie bosses you about, you tell her that you are the boss, and that she needs to sit on the NAUGHTY STEP for five minutes."

"Well…" Mother gulped. "I will try. Ahem." The lady cleared her throat. "Bonnie darling? Would you mind awfully sitting on this perfectly ordinary step here for a moment?"

CATACLYSMICALLY NAUGHTY

RIDICULOUSLY NAUGHTY

NAUGHTY

"NO!" shouted her daughter. "You sit on the NAUGHTY STEP right now or I am going to make you sleep in the shed for the rest of your miserable life!"

As quickly as her little legs could carry her, Mother raced

down the stairs and sat on the NAUGHTY STEP.

"PATHETIC!" sneered **WONDERNANNY**. The woman called up to Father. "And you are going to stand for this, are you, Mr Bonnington?"

"I most certainly am, yes," replied the timid little man. "Now, if you don't mind, I might just pop out to walk the dog."

Mother looked up at him, confused. "We don't have a dog!"

"Oh, well, I will go and buy one, then," replied the man, rushing down the stairs. "Excuse me…"

WONDERNANNY blocked his path. "You stay right there, you wretched excuse for a human being!"

"Am I in **trouble, WONDERNANNY?**" he asked, close to tears.

"You both are!" snapped the lady. "Mr and Mrs Bonnington, the pair of you are weak,

weak, weak!"

"Sorry," they both chimed in together.

"Don't say sorry! That is a sign of weakness!"

"Sorry!"

"Stop saying sorry!"

"Sorry!" the pair replied.

"Sorry, *WONDERNANNY,*" said Father. "We just can't stop saying sorry."

"Right! Down to business! I want the pair of you pitiful creatures to work together as a team to get your daughter to sit on the NAUGHTY STEP right NOW!"

"How on earth are we going to do that?" asked Mother.

"Yes? How are they going to do that?" asked Bonnie with a smirk. The little girl was enjoying herself.

"Like this," replied *WONDERNANNY* with an even bigger smirk. She hadn't called herself *WONDERNANNY* for nothing! The lady put her bulbous nose right up against the girl's, and her voice took on a dark and sinister tone. "If you don't do what I say, then THIS will be your new pet. It can even sleep in your bed with you at night!"

WONDERNANNY reached into her pocket and took out the biggest, hairiest **tarantula** in the world.

"Eurgh! NO!" shrieked Bonnie.

"I **hate** spiders!"

"I know!" **purred** the lady. "I have done my research on you!"

She dangled the poisonous creature right in front of the girl's **eyes.**

"STOP! STOP!"

pleaded Bonnie. "I'll do whatever you say! Whatever!"

"Then sit on the

NAUGHTY STEP!"

Bonnie couldn't get there fast enough. She shoved her parents out of the way and plonked herself down on the NAUGHTY STEP. Although she hadn't been asked to, Bonnie crossed her arms and sat up straight to give the impression that she was, in fact, one of the world's **best** children.*

"See, young lady?" snarled *WONDERNANNY.* "That wasn't SOOOO hard, was it?"

She put the spider back in her pocket.

"Now what?" asked Bonnie.

"I don't want to hear a **peep** out of you for at least an hour. Not a **peep!** Do you **understand** me?"

Bonnie nodded her head. She was determined not to let out a **peep** of any kind.

From the balustrade above, Benji let his yo-yo uncurl down and hit his sister on the head.

DONK!

"OW!" she cried.

"I said not a **peep!**" repeated *WONDERNANNY.*

"Now, young Master Benji Bonnington, I am leaving **you** in charge!"

The boy smiled to himself.

* *The World's Best Children* would be a really boring book.

He had waited his **whole** life for this moment.

"Mr and Mrs Bonnington, I need to speak to you in private. Follow me into the lounge! Quickly! No dawdling! **Chop-chop!**"

The pair did what they were told, and followed the lady through the doorway as **fast** as they could. My word, this lady meant business!

The yo-yo came down again.

And again.

DONK!

DONK!

And again!

DONK!

In fact, it hit Bonnie on the head a few hundred times before the hour was up. If the girl made even the faintest noise, a voice from the lounge would shout,

"NOT A **PEEP!**"

Eventually the hour was up, and Bonnie's parents came back into the hallway with smiles on their faces. **WONDERNANNY** had given them a whole armoury of dreaded things to keep their daughter from being a **bossyboots** in case she grew accustomed to the tarantula. Just the threat of any one of these should keep Bonnie's bossiness in check.

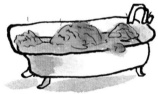

"Do you want me to bury your **hairdryer** in the garden?"

"NO!"

"Your bath is ready! Filled to the brim with the greenest, gloopiest **snot.**"

"NOO!"

"You can eat your dinner **without** tomato ketchup tonight."

"NOOO!"

"I thought you liked **raw** turnips for tea."

"NOOOO!"

"I have put a nice movie on for you to watch before you go to bed. It's all about a **vampire** who tap, tap, taps on children's bedroom windows at night. Don't have nightmares! Tap, tap, tap! What's that noise?"

"NOooo!"

"I thought this week you could put the

duvet back inside the duvet cover yourself."

"NOOoooo!"

"What's that smell? I washed all your clothes in **cats' pee.**

That way at school everyone will know you are coming."

"NOOOoooo!"

"We swapped your bedrooms while you were out, so now

your little brother has the **biggest** room."

"NOOOOoooo!"

"I thought you wanted your pocket money

to go to children **less** fortunate than yourself."

"NOOOOOoooo!"

And the absolute worst of the worst...

"We have been talking, and we know

all the kids in your year have one, but

we have decided it is best we don't

buy you a mobile phone for your

birthday. In fact, we think you should

wait until you are at least FORTY!"

"NOOOOOOOoo!"

So, when **WONDERNANNY** left the Bonnington household at the end of the day, she gave a very special present to the family.

"Well, my work here is **done!** Another triumph for **WONDERNANNY!** Ha! Ha! Now, I thought I would leave the nice little hairy **tarantula** here. It needs a good home." She looked over to Bonnie, who was **aghast.**

Without saying a word, Benji opened up his hands and the lady passed it to him. Bonnie let out a silent **scream** as her little brother stroked the creature.

"Here's my card," said **WONDERNANNY** as she turned to go. "It's got all my details on there if you need to follow up. Goodbye, Bonnie, it was so... **wonderful** to meet you." She smirked to herself. She had won again.

WONDERNANNY!
WONDERNANNY'S
WONDERLAND WN100
CALL NOW!

As soon as the front door closed behind the lady and her team, Benji announced, "I **love** spiders."

Mother and Father were thrilled that their son had finally uttered his first words, aged ten.

"In fact, I love spiders so much that this deadly tarantula can stay in my room. Unless you would prefer it to cuddle up with you, Bonnie?"

"No. No. No. No. No. And once again **no!**" snapped the girl. "Benji, do you actually LOVE spiders?"

"Yep!" replied the boy brightly. "They are my favourite."

The girl's face darkened. "It wasn't you who was putting them in my bed every night, was it, Benji? **BENJI?**"

The boy kept his cool. "Well, I'd better put **Bossypants** to bed," he replied, artfully avoiding the answer.

"**Bossypants?**" sneered the girl. "What kind of a name is that for a spider?"

"I named it after **you.** Goodnight!"

*

A week later, Bonnie's episode of **WONDERNANNY** was shown on television, and the whole family sat on the sofa together to watch it. That was a first. Normally Bonnie would lie flat on the sofa as the other three were forced to sit on the floor. Mother, Father and Benji all howled with laughter at seeing Bonnie get her comeuppance on national television.

"HA! HA! HA!"

Bonnie simply **scowled.**

On the television, **WONDERNANNY** signed off the episode with a piece to camera. "Knowing your children's worst nightmares is **key** in keeping their bad behaviour in check, just like we found with that nasty little Bonnie Bonnington. One threat of being bitten by a fatally poisonous spider and she is now good as gold. We all have fears. My biggest fear, believe it or not, is not spiders but **cheese!** Yes, I can't stand the smell of it. It makes me want to **hurl**. Goodnight!"

A light bulb flickered on in Bonnie's brain.

DING!

Bonnie became hell-bent on revenge. She wanted to teach that awful **WONDERNANNY** a lesson she would never forget. Immediately, she began secretly stockpiling cheese. The smellier the better. Not just cheese cheese, from her classmates' sandwiches at school, or bits from the bin at the supermarket. Oh no. Bonnie collected **FOOT CHEESE*** too.

Bonnie kept all her precious **cheese** in the shed at the end of the garden so it would not arouse suspicion.

PONGTASTIC

* FOOT CHEESE is so PONGTASTIC even the French don't eat it.

When she had filled the shed, she found the card
WONDERNANNY had left with her parents in a drawer,
which had her home address on it. Bonnie waited until
dark and then filled the wheelbarrow three metres
high with **cheese**, before trundling
down the streets to find
WONDERNANNY'S house.

WHIRR!

WHIRR!

WHIRR!

Unsurprisingly, the huge TV star lived in a huge mansion, which she had named **"WONDERNANNY'S WONDERLAND".** It seemed there was **money** to be made in naughty children.

Bonnie could see the lady's shadow moving around inside. She crept up to the house, but found that all the doors and windows were locked.

"BLAST!" said Bonnie to herself. However, parked in the driveway was **WONDERNANNY'S** brand-new Bentley. Fortunately for Bonnie, one of the car windows was very slightly open at the top, so Bonnie began squeezing the cheese through the gap. The girl worked through the night. The smelly cheese o o z e d into the car, filling it up to the height of the steering wheel. It took hours to put in everything that was piled up on the wheelbarrow, but Bonnie managed it.

Now dawn was breaking and, as the girl lay in wait behind a bush, a half-asleep **WONDERNANNY** waddled over

to her car. Without looking, she slid in, only to find herself up to her armpits in **cheese**.

"ARGH!" screamed the lady.

Bonnie leaped out from her hiding place and jumped on to the bonnet of the Bentley. **CLONK!**

"Sorry, *WONDERNANNY*, did you say you did or didn't like **cheese?**" shouted the girl.

"BONNIE!" shouted the lady. But before she could utter another word her face turned a violent shade of **green**. Then, true to her word, she hurled, spraying the inside of the windscreen with a putrid yellow liquid.

"BLEURGH!" SPLATTER!

Bonnie smirked. *"WONDERNANNY better watch out when naughty children are about!"*

She leaped down from the bonnet of the Bentley, and ran all the way home, chuckling to herself with every step.

The smirk, however, didn't last too long, as that evening **WONDERNANNY** sent over a huge package to the Bonnington household. It read **"FRAGILE"** on the outside. When Mother and Father opened it, they saw the box was full of hundreds and hundreds of deadly **spiders.** The label read:

SOME FRIENDS FOR BOSSYPANTS. ENJOY! WITH LOVE, WONDERNANNY X

There were far too many spiders for Benji to look after himself, so, very **kindly,** he let a hundred or so cuddle up at night with his darling sister.

"ARGH!"

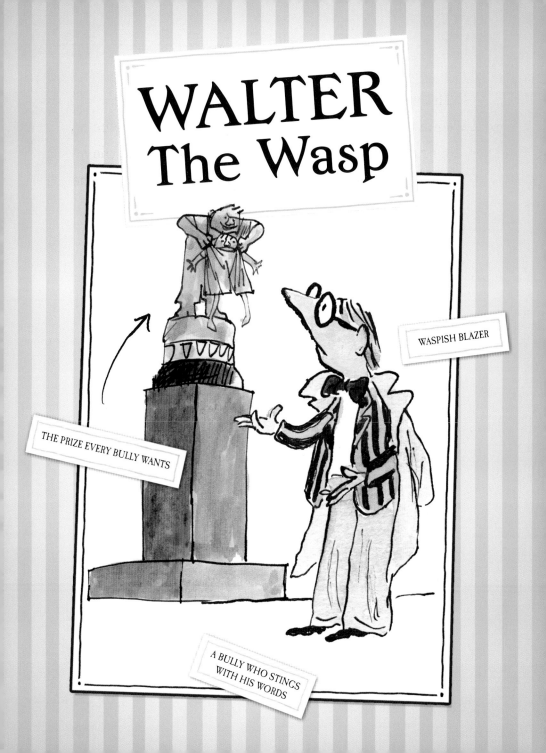

WALTER
The Wasp

WASPISH BLAZER

THE PRIZE EVERY BULLY WANTS

A BULLY WHO STINGS
WITH HIS WORDS

WALTER
the Wasp

WALTER WAS AN unlikely bully. He was unusually short for his age, wore black-rimmed glasses and was always flamboyantly dressed with a velvet bow tie and a natty yellow-and-black blazer. Walter never hit anyone – instead he would **hurt** people with his *insults*.

His tongue was like a **wasp's tail:** it could deliver a painful sting. The boy was a master at making up cruel nicknames for people.

His Spanish teacher, Mr Gari, who was bald, Walter named **"Garibaldi"**.

A teacher with a beard became simply **"The Gnome"**.

For the wide Miss Tink he gave the nickname **"Miss Tank"**.

The flappy-eared Art teacher became **"Ear-Wings"**.

The hairy PE teacher was dubbed **"Caveman"**.

Dr Trunter became **"Dr Grunter"** as he always blew off when he bent over to pick up a pen.

Miss May, who couldn't control her class, became **"Miss Mayhem"**.

The long-armed librarian became **"the Orang-utan"**.

The sweaty Head of Science he named **"Puddles"**, as that is what he had under his arms.

Mr Fump the Woodwork teacher, who'd sawn off one of his fingers in a woodworking accident, became **"Fump the Stump"**.

Walter was a wit who had an answer for everything. This infuriated his teachers.

When his Maths teacher asked him, "If I have six apples in one hand, and seven in the other, what do I have?"…

"Big hands," replied Walter in his withering drawl.

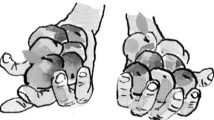

When a teacher asked, "Why don't any of you **ever** answer my questions?" Walter quipped, "You are the teacher – I was rather hoping you would know."

One morning, the headmistress enquired, "Walter, why are you late?"

The boy answered, "I was merely obeying the *sign*."

"Which sign, boy?"

"School ahead. Go slow."

"Are you having trouble hearing?" demanded another teacher.

"No, sir. I am having trouble *listening*," replied Walter with a roll of his eyes.

"If five people all gave you five thousand pounds, what would you have?"

"A private-school education," Walter purred.

"Walter! Why on earth are you writing your multiplications on the floor?"

"But, sir, you told me not to use tables."

"Walter! Where's your exercise book?"

"At home, miss."

"What is it doing there?"

"Having a *much* better time than me."

"Walter, how do you change centimetres to metres?"

"Cut out the 'centi' part. *Easy-peasy, pudding and pie!*"

"If you place a slide under the microscope and can't see anything, what might the problem be, Walter?"

"You are *blind*, perhaps?"

"Sir, I regret to inform you that *the dog*
ate my homework," announced Walter.

"You expect me to believe that?"
thundered the teacher. "Why would your
dog eat your homework?"

"Perhaps if I had smeared it with dog food first...?"

Such was the power of Walter's dark wit that soon
everyone in his school had been on the receiving end of
his verbal slap-downs. One day, the headmistress, Mrs
Cankle, spotted Walter tormenting a younger boy who
had an unusually large nose.

"Roger?" purred Walter.

"What now, Walter?"

"Does your nose always arrive
five minutes *before* you do?"

"WALTER!
There you are!"
interrupted the
headmistress,
wearing her favourite
purple dress.

"Mrs Cankle, why are you dressed as a Quality Street?"

"Walter, I and the teachers have been talking, and we would like to put you forward for the BULLY OF THE YEAR competition."

"Pray tell me more..." replied Walter, his eyes lighting up at the thought of winning a prize for his cruelty.

"The BULLY OF THE YEAR competition has been running for the past hundred years," said Mrs Cankle. "Many of the world's worst children come from all over the planet to take part."

All of these children shared a dream, to be crowned BULLY OF THE YEAR. If they won, they got to lift the solid gold statuette, which depicts a bully giving a smaller child a wedgie.*

Much like the Olympics, the competition is hosted by a different nation each year. It all takes place in a stadium in front of a huge booing crowd. A panel of judges marks the competitors in a number of events.

* A wedgie happens when a bully holds up their victim by their trousers, or, even worse, by their underpants. Ouch!

These include:

Name-calling (Walter's particular area of expertise)

Blowing off on someone's head

Hair-yanking

Ear-pulling

Foot-stamping

Arm-pinching

Bog-washing (This is the bully's favourite: lifting their victim up by their ankles, putting their head down a toilet and then flushing.)

Tickling until a little bit of wee comes out

Bogey-flicking

Book-hurling

Spamming (This is the ancient art of slapping someone on the forehead.)

Over the years, there have been many famous winners, all legendary figures in the bullying world.

Who can forget OLEG THE OPPRESSOR? He won the very first BULLY OF THE YEAR competition in 1905.

Oleg was a boy from Siberia who put fear into the hearts of all the millions of children across Russia. Only twelve, he already had a thick, bushy beard. He terrorised his victims by spinning them round by their legs and then **hurling** them huge distances. Sometimes they would land many miles away.

"Me Oleg. You flying through air."   **"ARGH!"**

Some years later the statue was lifted by INGRID THE INTIMIDATOR. All the way from Sweden, Ingrid was an expert at making the largest snowballs known to mankind. They were **bigger** than most snowmen.

Such was Ingrid's strength that she could hurl these snowballs at terrific speed. From a distance of up to a mile away, Ingrid could easily

knock a child out cold.   **"OOF!"**

"Thank you, thank you! They should come round in a couple of hours."

Also in the BULLY OF THE YEAR hall of fame is
TAKUMI THE TERRORISER. Takumi was
from Japan and a highly skilled sumo wrestler.
Only ten years old, he ate a **tonne** of raw fish
every day. As a result, he was much
bigger and **heavier** than his
grown-up opponents. He bullied
his victims by sitting on them
until their faces went blue.

"Do you **surrender?**"

"URGH!"

WANG WANG THE WHACKER was from
nearby China. Wang Wang might have been
only three feet tall, but she was an expert
in martial arts. Her signature move was
to twirl two bamboo sticks at terrific
speed before **whacking** people on
their bottoms with them.

"TAKE **THAT!** AND THAT!
AND **THAT!**"

"Ouch! OUCH! OOOUUUCH!"

Many years later, the BULLY OF THE YEAR competition was won by a Spanish boy named TAURO THE TORMENTOR. Tauro fancied himself as a champion bullfighter, and tormented the children in his school playground in much the same way bullfighters torment bulls. He would swirl his red cape in their faces and then jump on their backs when they tried to run away, much to the disapproval of the crowd.

"RUN, LITTLE BULL! RUN!"

"OW! You are heavy!"

The winner last year was named BAM-BAM THE BOOMERANG BOY. You might think from his name that Bam-Bam was good at throwing boomerangs. No, he just had a really large heavy one with which he would bash his victims over the head.

"OW! STOP THAT!"

"Bam-Bam thinks it's funny."

"It's not!"

"Bam-Bam thinks it is."

It was difficult to say who was happier that Walter was missing a week at school to take part: Walter, or **everyone** at his school. They were delighted to see the back of him. So off Walter flew to Rio, to represent Great Britain at the BULLY OF THE YEAR competition.

Walter had two main rivals.

The first was Thumper the Thumper. She was a girl with unusually large hands and feet from America. When she clenched her fists, they were the size of footballs. Because Thumper's arms were so very LONG, when she went to thump someone in the playground, normally another **dozen**

children would be

knocked **out**

in the process.

She could propel her arms at such a **speed** that when Thumper was in full **thumping** mode they became a blur. Thumper's **thumping** was merciless.

Anyone, anything, any time could set her off on a **thumping** spree:

Anyone whom she thought had given her a **"funny look"**…

Spotting someone reading a **book** meant they were "a swot" who deserved "a good **thumping**"…

Anyone named Colin. Especially **girls**…

Children who owned **hamsters**…

Children who didn't own **hamsters**…

Anyone who **sneezed** within a hundred-metre radius of her…

Boys who wore **glasses**…

People with **spots**…

Girls who wore hair **scrunchies,** even though Thumper wore them herself…

Kids who had smelly **egg sandwiches** in their lunchbox…

Science-fiction enthusiasts…

Chess players…

Anyone who expressed even a vague interest in **badminton**…

The second rival was from France. Pierre **le Pooh** was famous for his **horrendous breath**. He took delight in eating the stinkiest French cheeses and then burping violently into the faces of his victims. This would make them:

Faint...

Cry...

Hurl...

Run...

Strip naked and **burn** all their clothes...

Leap into a lake to try to get the **smell off**...

Move to New Zealand...

Lock themselves in a darkened room and not come out for ten years...

Jump into a sheep dip...

Go through a **car wash** without a car...

Walter did well in all the heats, and soon found himself in the final three with **Thumper** and Pierre. Now there was just a handful of events left to decide which of them would be crowned the BULLY OF THE YEAR.

The first event was "Make your teacher cry". Walter, **Thumper** and Pierre took their places on the start line as the crowd of thousands in the stadium b o o e d .

Being bullies, they lapped up the boos, and even smiled and waved to the crowd. They knew they were hated, and they enjoyed it.

"BOoOoOoOoo!"

Seated at a desk ahead of them was a teacher, a painfully shy Geography teacher named Mr Coy. The man was **quietly** getting on with some marking.

BANG! The adjudicator shot the starter pistol, and Thumper and Pierre rushed at the teacher. Walter strolled towards him, as if he had all the time in the world. Before Walter could utter a word, or Pierre could summon a burp, Thumper **thumped** the desk... **CRUMP!**

...sending all the marking f l u t t e r i n g into the air. She thumped the desk so hard that it left a huge fist-shaped dent in the table. The poor teacher was startled but **not** in tears.

This was Pierre's chance. From the depths of his tummy, he started forcing a **cheesy** burp out.

"BUUUUURRRRP!"

A cloud of green gas **EXPLODED** into the face of the teacher. The man coughed and spluttered, and his eyes moistened. The adjudicator peered in to see if this was a win.

"I'm **not** crying," spluttered Mr Coy. "I just have something in my eye."

Now Walter could go in for the kill.

"Geography teacher, are you?" he purred.

"Y-y-yes?" replied the teacher.

"It would be wonderful if you could... get **lost!"**

Silence descended upon the stadium.

Poor Mr Coy's feelings had been **hurt.** A tear welled in his eye and r o l l e d down his cheek.

The steward saw this and announced over a loudhailer,

"Walter is the **winner!"**

The crowd all jeered.

"BOO!"

A smug smile spread across Walter's face, and he straightened his bow tie and did a little bow. This just made them **boo** more loudly.

"BOoo!"

The next event was called "Torment the dinner lady". Whoever the panel of judges decided had tormented the poor woman the most despicably would be the **winner.** The tormenting could be done in whatever way the bully wanted, as long as it was nasty.

A dinner lady named Mrs Spatt stood waiting behind a counter of inedible school food. Boiled cabbage that had turned to MUSH, mince that had gone mouldy and a trifle with fruit so off and fizzy that the layers of cream and jelly above it were bubbling like molten lava. Mrs Spatt was used to having her food treated as if children would rather flush it straight down the toilet than eat it.

BANG!

As the starter pistol went off, the dinner lady grimaced and picked up her weighty metal ladle. A ladle with which she delighted in **rapping** children on the knuckles.

TORMENT THE
DINNER LADY

Walter cleared his throat to speak. "Spatt by name, and spat—"

"**Don't bother,** dear!" she snapped. "I've heard it **all** before."

The crowd cheered the dinner lady, and she held her ladle aloft in victory. This allowed Pierre to seize his moment and belch his cheesy French burp straight into her face.

"BURP!"

For a moment, it looked like the burp might have knocked her out cold, but as soon as the smell had snaked up her nose Mrs Spatt actually **smiled.**

"Smells like one of my delicious cheese pies! Ha! **Ha!**" she laughed.

The crowd roared their approval.

This left only **Thumper.** The mighty competitor from the US thumped her hand down on the counter. Plates flew through the air and smashed on the ground.

CRASH!

The bowl of trifle took off too, and the molten-lava-like dessert landed right in Mrs Spatt's face.

"ARGH!" she screamed.

"The fruit is so **rancid** it's actually taking my skin off!"

The lady hitched up her skirt and ran across the stadium where she was hosed down by some waiting firemen. The water shot out of their hoses so **fast** that Mrs Spatt was suspended in the air by the jets, though she was happy to land in the arms of a hunky firefighter.

Thumper looked on with glee, as the crowd all booed her. **"BOO!"**

Being a bully, of course **Thumper** lapped it up.

Now it was time for the final event. This was the "Steal the pocket money from the small child". Whichever of the bullies pocketed the coin was the winner.

A **small child** entered the stadium to huge cheers from the crowd. His name was Otto, and he couldn't have been more than six years old. He held aloft a gold coin, which he then carefully placed in his pocket. The steward ushered him into position as the judges looked on eagerly.

STEAL THE POCKET MONEY FROM THE SMALL CHILD

The three champion bullies all stood on the starting line, smug looks on their faces.

"This is going to be so **easy**," said Thumper.

"Easy-peasy, pudding and pie!" added Walter.

"One **cheesy** burp and that coin is mine!" uttered Pierre.

BANG!

The starter pistol went off. The three bullies circled little Otto.

Without saying a word, **Thumper** picked the little boy up by his ankles and began to shake him so the coin would fall out of his pocket.

"Gimme your pocket money!" she demanded.

"No," stated Otto firmly.

"Then I'm going to **thump** you!" she shouted, holding him by one ankle, and clenching her huge fist.

"Not if I thump you first!" said the boy. He clenched his fist, and **Thumper** immediately dropped him in terror.

"Not the face! Not the **face!**"

she screamed. The girl hid behind

Walter, even though she was about

twice the size of him.

The crowd in the stadium all

clapped and cheered the little boy.

"HOORAY!"

As Otto picked himself up from the

ground, Pierre went in for the **kill.**

He took a deep inhalation of breath,

but before he could expel it Otto cupped his hand,

broke **wind** into it...

PFTT!

...and **WAFTED** it in the bully's

direction.

WAFT!

Pierre's face turned a putrid shade

of green.

"*Non! Non! Non!*"

he shouted.

"I think I am going to... how you say... puke?"

Indeed he did, all over **Thumper**.

SPLUuUuRT!

"EURGH!" cried the girl.

Again the crowd went wild

for brave little Otto.

"HoOrAy!"

Now it was Walter's turn. What could he

say to part the little squirt from his pocket money?

"You are so small, you must have posed for the

trophy!" he snickered. "Ha! **Ha!** Give me your pocket

money now or I will have everyone in this stadium

laughing at **YOU!**"

"Here it is!" said Otto, taking the coin out of his

pocket.

The crowd all gasped. What was the boy up to?

Walter turned to the crowd, and held out his

hand towards Otto. He had **won.** Or so he

thought.

The audience all booed Walter.

"BOoo!"

Without Walter seeing, Otto squirted a tiny splurge of **superglue** on one side of the coin. Then, as Walter turned back to take the coin, Otto pressed it on to the end of the bully's nose. Walter's eyes **crossed** as he saw what had happened.

Immediately, he tried to take it **off.**

He **pulled.**

And **TUGGED.**

And **YANKED.**

But, however hard he tried, the coin just **wouldn't** budge.

"Don't worry," said Otto.

"People will just think you have a giant drawing pin on your nose."

"**HA!** HA! **HA!**" went the crowd, h o o t i n g with laughter at Walter. They were absolutely loving it. The world had never seen a BULLY OF THE YEAR final like this. As for Walter, he burst into floods of tears.

"**BOO!**

HOO!

HOO!"

Otto couldn't help but smile. The little boy had given these awful bullies a taste of their own medicine, and – surprise, surprise – they didn't like it **one bit.**

The steward presented the competition trophy to Otto. The boy read the inscription out loud, "BULLY OF THE YEAR?"

He held the trophy high above his head...

"No, thank you!"

...before **smashing** it to the ground as hard as he could, breaking it into a million pieces.

SMASH!

CLANK!

CLINK!

CLUNK!

With that, Otto strolled out of the stadium. Every single person in the crowd rose to their feet, and clapped and **cheered** the boy.

"HOORAY!"

The bits of the trophy were thrown in the **bin,** which is of course where bullying belongs.

Kung Fu
KYLIE

KYLIE WAS A girl who loved **whacking** people.
Whacking people indiscriminately is guaranteed to earn
you a place in a book about the world's worst children.

The girl spent all her time playing beat-'em-up
computer games, and watching kung fu films. Diligently
she studied all the moves, and practised
them in her bedroom mirror.

Kylie had no formal training in **martial arts,** but that didn't stop her from dressing in white pyjamas, tying a black sock round her head and going everywhere barefoot.

In no time, Kylie had kung-fued the three toughest boys in her school.

A flying chop was enough to make Biggie scream for mercy.

"HI-YA!" shouted Kylie.

"Nooo!"

A cartwheel kick put an end to the Plopper's glittering career in bullying.

"HI-YA!"

"HELP!"

And a **poke** on the nose reduced
Pongo to a **g i b b e r i n g** wreck.

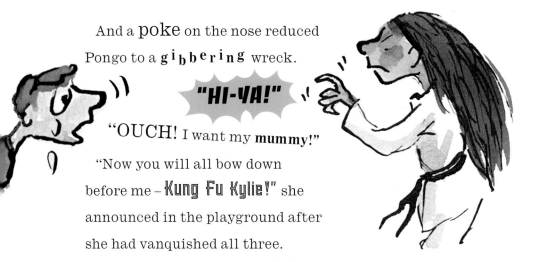

"HI-YA!"

"OUCH! I want my **mummy!**"

"Now you will all bow down
before me – **Kung Fu Kylie!**" she
announced in the playground after
she had vanquished all three.

Next, she turned her **martial-arts** skills on her teacher.

When Mr Twig gave her an **F** in his Geography test,
Kung Fu Kylie leaped off the top of the lockers...

"HI-YA!"

...giving him a **chop** on the **chops**.

"ARGH!" yelled the teacher,
and promptly changed the
mark to an **A***.

Setting homework is something that the girl's Maths teacher, Mrs Plimplam, is unlikely to ever do again. The last time she tried, Kung Fu Kylie did a spinning **kick,** sending her worksheets scattering into the air.

"NOOOOOO!"

"HI-YA!"

cried Mrs Plimplam, chasing after them.

"My precious babies!"

And when the dinner lady, Mrs Mung, didn't serve up enough chips for Kylie – and Kylie really, **really** loved chips – she was dispatched across the dining hall on one of her own food trollies.

"HI-YA!"

"GOOOODBYYYYYEEEEE!"

Kylie's own family was not safe from her kung fu.

When her grandfather wanted to watch snooker rather than cartoons, Kylie announced, "Prepare to meet thy **doom**, Grandpa Ted!"

POW!

"Ow! Here's the remote!"

Another night, Kylie's mother was munching her way through a box of her favourite chocolates, and refusing to share.

"Mother! Bow down before the mighty power of me, the chosen one! Giveth me the *walnut whirl!*"

"Never!"

THWACK!

"Argh! Kylie!

You **horrible** girl!

Now me chocolates have gone everywhere!"

The family cat would be minding its own business, curled up on the armchair where Kylie wanted to sit.

"Take that, Tiddlywinks!"

"M M M I I A A O O W W W !"

BAM!

screamed the cat as it jumped out of the way of her kung fu chop just in time.

No one was safe. Not even complete strangers. Kung Fu Kylie soon became famous in her little town of Dollop for being absolutely the worst child who had ever lived there. She was a one-girl crimewave, bringing pain and destruction wherever she went. PC Shod, the local policeman, recorded 317 "incidents of a kung fu nature".

Kylie made the front page of the local paper, the **Dollop Gazette**, hundreds of times.

Dollop Gazette

BREAKS TOE
KUNG FU KYLIE KICKS OVER BURGER VAN IN DISPUTE OVER KETCHUP AND BREAKS TOE IN PROCESS

Dollop Gazette

LANDS IN WEDDING CAKE
KUNG FU MENACE CRASHES THROUGH GOLF-CLUB WINDOW WHEN DENIED ENTRY

Dollop Gazette

KUNG FU KYLIE FLIES THROUGH LOCAL LIBRARY
Felled by quick-thinking librarian and *Lord of the Rings* in hardback

Dollop Gazette

GIRL DOES KUNG FU CHOP ON VICAR
DURING CHRISTENING OF LITTLE SISTER BECAUSE SHE FINDS IT BORING – ENDS UP IN FONT.

Dollop Gazette

KUNG FU KYLIE FOUND IN POND
AS ATTACK ON NOISY DUCK GOES BADLY WRONG

CHINA SHOP DESTROYED
NO REWARD GIVEN FOR NAMING WHO IS RESPONSIBLE.
IT'S KYLIE!

Dollop Gazette

LOLLIPOP LADY
WHACKED ON BOTTOM WITH OWN LOLLIPOP STICK
BAREFOOT GIRL IN PYJAMAS WITH A SOCK TIED ROUND HER HEAD SEEN FLEEING THE SCENE.

Dollop Gazette

PRICELESS PAINTING
DESTROYED
ON A SCHOOL TRIP WHEN KUNG FU KYLIE KICKS THROUGH IT! KYLIE'S POUND-A-WEEK POCKET MONEY IS FROZEN. "IT'S GOING TO TAKE HER THOUSANDS OF YEARS TO PAY IT OFF," SAYS MOTHER.

KUNG FU GIRL ATTACKS POSTBOX IN A RAGE
KUNG FU KYLIE COMES A CROPPER AT HAVING MISSED POST. POSTBOX WINS!

Gazette

WONKY HAND
HAIRLINE CRACK FOUND IN STONE STATUE IN TOWN SQUARE. KUNG FU KYLIE ADMITTED TO HOSPITAL WITH WONKY HAND.

Gazette

This had to **stop.** So one day the town's mayor, Mrs Plunk, called an emergency meeting of all the people of Dollop in the town hall.

The entire population of the town turned out. There was standing room only in the hall. Every single one of them had suffered at the girl's hands (and feet) and wanted an end to Kung Fu Kylie's reign of terror.

"I am begging you, the good people of Dollop, for help in putting an end to this one-girl kung fu crimewave!" called out the mayor.

The place erupted.

"Drag her through a gorse bush backwards!" yelled the local florist, whose entire stock of flowers had been destroyed when

Kylie used them for thumping practice.

"Burn the witch at the **stake!"** shouted a little old lady named Mrs Tog, who in a scuffle with Kylie over the last doughnut in the bakery had been kung fu kicked and landed head first in a banana cream pie. That was last year and to this day she still stinks of bananas.

"Burn her at the **stake?"** boomed the vicar. "Have you gone stark raving mad, woman? This is the twenty-first century!"

"I am sorry, Reverend," muttered Mrs Tog, a little bit ashamed of herself.

The vicar continued: "That girl needs to be

hung, drawn and **quartered!"**

The whole place erupted into wild cheers.

"YES!"

A lone voice could be heard against the **tsunami** of fury.

"Please! Please! Hunging, drawning and **quarterering** belongs in the **past!**" It was unusual for the local newsagent, Raj, to be the voice of reason, but it was indeed his voice they were hearing. Eventually the town hall fell silent.

"Thank you, folk of Dollop. We are talking about a ten-year-old girl here! And one of my best customers, so I can't afford to lose the business!"

"Oh, that's what it's all about!" shouted Mrs Tog.

"Burn her and **then hang, draw** and **quarter** her!"**

"YES!" shouted the crowd.
"NO!" shouted Raj.
"Kung Pu Kylie just needs to be taught a lesson!"

"But how?" asked the mayor.

"Yes, how?" murmured the crowd.

"Beat the little rascal at her **own game!** Now, good people of Dollop, I myself am a man of peace. I wouldn't even hurt a fly, even if I did catch it shoplifting. Does anyone here know how to do this kung pu?"

The townsfolk all looked at each other blankly.

"I am an expert in *crochet*," announced Mrs Tog.

"I dabble in origami," added Mrs Plimplam.

"I once had some *sushi*," piped up PC Shod. "Though I didn't like it. Does that count?"

The crowd murmured their disapproval as Raj continued. "If one of us trained up as a kung pu master, then the girl would at last have someone who can **stop** her!"

"But **who?**"

demanded Mayor Plunk.

"Maybe we can all draw a **straw!**" said Raj. "I brought a packet from my shop." True to his word, the newsagent produced a sorry set of straws. "I have them on special offer as a dog chewed them, and you can't suck through them any more. Apart from that, they are in **mint** condition. If everyone can put in just five pence, then—"

"There isn't time for all that nonsense, Raj!" announced Mayor Plunk. "You can do it!"

"Do what?" asked Raj.

"Learn kung fu!"

The town hall erupted into cheers.

"B-b-but I don't know any kung pu!" he protested. Needless to say, the newsagent was mightily reluctant.

"That's all settled, then!" announced the mayor. "Raj has volunteered to take on Kung Fu Kylie. Three cheers for Raj. **Hip hip!**"

"Sorry, I—" interjected Raj.

The crowd pretended not to hear him.

"HOORAY!"

"Hip hip!" continued the mayor.

"I never said—"

"Hip hip!"

"HoORAY!"

"I **really** don't think I can—"

"HoORAY!"

"And one for luck!"

"PLEASE!"

"HoORAY!"

The good people of Dollop started filing out of the town hall, patting their local newsagent on the back.

"Good for you, Raj!"

"Good luck, Raj. You will **need it!**"

"Don't worry, Raj. I will come and visit you in **hospital.**"

The poor newsagent was left alone in the hall, contemplating his fate. "Oh golly gosh!" he muttered to himself.

The next morning, he stripped down to his vest and pants in his shop, and began training. He drew a huge **R** on his vest.

"I am  SUPER RAJ!"

he told himself. The man was determined not to let the town down, and **threw** himself into training.

BAM!

The newsagent round-kicked a large bag of **marshmallows**, scattering the pink and white fluffy balls everywhere.

PING!

He placed a **jelly baby** on a chair, and stalked it from behind, before flicking it off with his finger.

He **slammed** his hand down on a chocolate orange, breaking it open in an instant.

KAPOW!

He ate the chocolate orange in a matter of seconds. *MUNCH. MUNCH. MUNCH.*
"Mmm. One of my **five a day**," he muttered.

He **tore** a copy of *Puzzler* magazine in two. Raj then hastily sticky-taped it together, so he could put it back on sale.

RIP!

PFFT!

Using **wind** from his bottom, he moved a toffee bonbon along the counter without even touching it.

He **sat** cross-legged on the floor of his shop as still as he could. He waited and waited until the fly that had been buzzing around his shop landed on his **nose**.

BUZZ!

Maybe he could hurt a fly, after all! As fast as a bolt of **lightning,** Raj whacked his nose with a rolled-up copy of *Vogue*…

…knocking himself **out** in the process.

BASH!

THUD!

DING!

The door to the newsagent's shop opened and Mayor Plunk rushed in.

"Raj! **RAJ?**" she shouted.

The lady slapped the man on the face to wake him up.

SLAP! SLAP! **SLAP!**

"**OW!**" said Raj.

"You are hurting me!"

"Why are you asleep in your shop, wearing only your **undercrackers?**" she asked. It was a reasonable question. A man in his pants selling food. It didn't seem hygienic.

"I was training to become SUPER RAJ!"

"And why have you got a flattened wine gum stuck to your bottom?"

"Oh, I must have been saving that for later!"

Raj peeled the wine gum off his underpants and offered it to Mayor Plunk. "Would you like half?"

"NO! I would **NOT!**"

The newsagent popped the sweet in his mouth. Immediately his face **soured**.

"Eurgh. I am not sure I like this new farty flavour. Yuck! Yuckety yuck yuck **yuck.**" Raj stuck the wine gum back on his bottom. "Now, how can I help you? Half a *Curly Wurly?* Some pick-your-own marshmallows? A toffee bonbon that has been warmed slightly by a gust of fragrant *WIND*?"

"No. No. **No.** Raj, the people of Dollop need you. Kung Fu Kylie is in the town square destroying everything in sight!"

Raj's face melted into an expression of fear.

"Oh no," he uttered.

"Oh **yes**. The girl is way out of control! She kung fu kicked a Portaloo over while a builder was sitting on it doing his **business**.

"HI-YA!"

The poor man was soaked from head to toe in **poo** juice!"

"Oh **double** no."

"Oh **yes**. Next, she turned her attention to her dinner lady, Mrs Mung.

She is currently hanging upside down from a lamppost, her **bloomers** flapping in the wind."

"Oh **triple** no."

"Oh **yes.** Then little old Mrs Tog just got **HURLED** over her shoulder and is now **stuck** up a tree!"

"Oh dear. Well, thank you so much for popping in. I must just tidy these tubes of sherbet. Good day!"

"No, Raj!" snapped Mayor Plunk. "You must stop Kung Fu Kylie. Now. PC Shod is trying his best, but he can't hold her off any longer!"

Just at that moment, the policeman came **slamming** into the shop window.

BASH!

WANG!

His face was flattened against the glass.

"I am terribly sorry," said Shod. "I just got **kung fu** kicked on my bottom and flew through the air." He slid down the glass, leaving a trail of **drool.**

"That window will need a **clean,**" muttered Raj.

"I hate to say this, because it must mean this town of ours is in **terrible** trouble, but, Raj, you are our only hope," announced Mayor Plunk.

Raj gulped. Then, as slowly as he possibly could, he walked out of his shop.

DING!

Ahead of him he saw public enemy number one: **Kung Fu Kylie**. The girl was standing on top of a double-decker bus she'd taken over. The passengers were all leaping out of the windows, trying to escape.

"Stop right there!" said Raj.

Kung Fu Kylie turned round. "Who said that?"

Raj hit the tree so hard that he **KNOCKED** himself out cold, and fell to the ground. The tree was **shaking**, and the little old lady who'd been hurled up into it, Mrs Tog, tumbled off her branch.

"ARGH!"

Fortunately for Mrs Tog (though unfortunately for Kylie),

she landed right

on top

of the

girl.

THUD!

"I am terribly sorry," said Mrs Tog, finding herself sitting on Kylie's **head.**

The townsfolk led by the mayor gathered all around, and were delighted to see that Kung Fu Kylie had been stopped in her tracks. She was now **PINNED** to the ground by an elderly lady.

"YES!" cheered the crowd.

"There will be no more kung fu, **young lady!**" announced the mayor. "Do you promise?"

There was no way out for the girl. "All right, all right, I promise!" said Kylie.

"Excellent!" said the mayor.

"YES!" shouted everyone.

The old lady released her grip, and the girl rose to her feet.

The noise of the crowd woke up Raj. Being **KNOCKED OUT** must have affected his memory, because he proclaimed,

"**SUPER RAJ** has **saved** the day!"

No one had the heart to tell him he **hadn't.**

The girl kept her fingers crossed behind her back.

"I **promise** not to do any more **kung fu.**"

"Good girl," said the mayor.

"Instead I am going to do **KARATE!** **HI-YA!**"
she yelled, sweeping her leg up to launch
a flying kick on the crowd.

As she did so, she slipped on Raj's
half-chewed and slobbery wine gum...

SLURP!

...and fell flat on her **bum**.

THUMP!!

"OW!"
she screamed.

Of course, the girl loved dishing out pain, but hated being on the receiving end.

Kylie burst into tears.

"Boo-hoo-hoo!"

Raj reached for a packet of tissues that he'd stuffed in the band of his **underpants.** "There, there, have a tissue," he said, proffering one.

"Thank you, Raj," sniffed the girl.

"That will be five p, please."

THE
END
*

* This is the final instalment in the trilogy. Or is it....?

from the desk of
David Walliams

Dear reader,

I was going to include you in *The World's Worst Children 3* collection, but, having spoken to your family, I have concluded that you are far too wicked to feature in this book. But don't think you've got off that lightly, because there might be another volume... just when you least expect it!

David Walliams